MONTHS AND OTHER STORIES

To Stanley Middleton, novelist

with gratitude

Also by Michael Standen

Start Somewhere (Heinemann)
A Sane and Able Man (Heinemann)
Stick-man (Heinemann)
The Dreamland Tree (Heinemann)
Over the Wet Lawn (Oxford University Press)
Time's Fly-Past (Flambard)

For: Pauline

MONTHS
AND OTHER STORIES

Michael Standen

Michael Standen

Sept. 1995

Published in 1994 by Flambard Press
4 Mitchell Avenue, Jesmond, Newcastle upon Tyne NE2 3LA

Flambard Press wishes to thank Northern Arts for its financial support.

Typeset by Pandon Press Ltd, Newcastle upon Tyne
Printed in Great Britain by Cromwell Press, Broughton Gifford,
Melksham, Wiltshire

A CIP catalogue record for this book is available from the British Library
ISBN 1 873226 12 8
© Michael Standen 1994

All rights reserved

Michael Standen has asserted his right
under the Copyright Designs and Patents Act, 1988
to be identified as the author of this work

CONTENTS

Preface   7

MONTHS

Ditching (*October 1914*)   11
Her Winning Ways (*November 1946*)   16
Reflected Glory (*December 1988*)   22
Getting Through (*January 1967*)   31
Saint Valentine on Tyne (*February 1990*)   36
This Side of Easter (*March 1956*)   43
Mixed Doubles (*April 1928*)   50
Tomorrow Is Another Day (*May 1961*)   59
Revelations (*June 1951*)   67
Too Close for Comfort (*July 19—*)   77
In Good Season (*August 1976*)   85
Light (*September 1905*)   95

OTHER STORIES

Driving Home   103
Beauty   108
Triptych   116
Dream   126

ACKNOWLEDGEMENTS

Some of these stories first appeared in *Stand* and *Iron*.

The illustrations used on the cover and in the text are by Peter Standen.

Under a Northern Arts scheme, the manuscript was prepared for publication at the Tyrone Guthrie Centre, Annaghmakerrig, Co. Monaghan.

PREFACE

A preface should tell the reader something not to be found in the work which the author hopes s/he is about to sink into. Famous tree-felling efforts by such as Wordsworth and Shaw ran to hectares. This is more in the nature of a foreword and refrains from rehearsing the history of the short story or speculating upon it as a form.

The bulk of this book is *Months*, a sequence of twelve stories covering between them most of the expiring century (1905–90). Oraries and Books of Hours were commissioned by great medieval patrons and some show the passing seasons month by month, so one imagines the limner or miniaturist going out every four or five weeks to fulfil his standing order. Now the ancient agricultural cycle has gone to pot (or to potash and worse) but months still mark the passage of time with their own weathers and vestigial festivities.

On a hint from a friend and with no Duc de Berry to bankroll the project, grew the simple idea of writing each month over a year a short story set in that month. Deadlines were not so much on the calendar as being the calendar itself. That year of 1989–90 became as long with the task as a small room enlarges itself when you paint it. A sustaining feature of the project was its simplicity; Chaucer's self-inflicted scheme in the *Canterbury Tales* was more ambitious but no less daft. And as the year wore on, the possibility that there were links of a sort, however subterranean, encouraged me, and about halfway through a grander recognition came. This could be my testimony to the century, my testament – no blockbuster but a little scruffy tessellated pavement, there perhaps to be discovered when the block bust.

Forewords are presumptuous and acknowledgements creep in of the 'without whom' variety, as if the worth of what follows is already acknowledged. A final important help in keeping the sequence going was another self-inflicted task on the part of Terrence Hardiman the actor, a friend from the age of eleven. His reading onto tape got the stories off the page and onto their feet, which is what the imagination of dear reader does – as authors scarcely dare to hope.

M.S.

MONTHS

DITCHING

OCTOBER 1914

'I'd as lief step on um.' Geoffrey Target's thirty-second birthday awakes to this, perfectly heard in his mind. Real hearing nets a fine tattoo of raindrops overhead, a sound with implications of what to do with the men. It is early though, still dark, so for a luxury he unwraps his scholar's mind from the oiled silk of more than ten years now and carefully applies it to Bob Farley.

Clinging to Bob's phrase is all of that day of months ago before the onset of the wonderful summer, a day from out of that patch of war fever, spring touch of Kaiser biliousness. Settling back head on bent arms, Geoffrey thinks he detects the first of sunrise pricking through wet canvas. Bob's hands had been resting a morning's ditching on his spade handle: behind him the white froth of thorn not quite done and buds of ash not quite open. Cutlass had been glad enough to stop too – good old boy with only a month or so to wheeze away but, tongue out and ears in business, trying to keep up doggy appearances.

I'd as lief step on um – yes, he's sure of the 'lief', Shakespearian, Germanic from *lieben*. Opening pronoun construction less exactly certain but 'step' had been uttered with the force of spadework. The final accusative was a scholarly crux – 'um' or 'him' or even 'en' – whatever it was, the reference was clearly to the imperious Hun. Knowledge of Middle English (which in truth had never been much sterner than a mental crush on his namesake, the Father of English Poetry) had somewhat deserted him. So much then for the text which resembled the scrappiest fragment of the *Greek Anthology*. Next he had been taught to consider questions of authenticity and authority. What, in all conscience, had made Bob Farley delve that up from some mental ditch? It had a strange authority. As Geoffrey recalled, there had been no preamble to the simple oracular comment. He knew that memory knitted its own patterns in the dark. Most likely was that the lad as he dug had mulled all morning over some newspaper reference to the Prince of princelings – it had been a week of field days for that sort of thing.

Evidence for that was clear. It had been all over the hoardings by the railway station, pictured now precisely, if not the mongered words thereon. Earlier that morning he had whistled Cutlass to stroll down for the purpose of seeing Stella off to Scotland. Her connection there was family money in the flabbergasting form of the relict of Findlay of Findlay, or something of that ilk. Poor girl. Her link with scholarship, with his studying days, was a dozen years ago and had come about through Wolfgang Stilz at college. The light is now suffusing the field tent, diluting darkness drop by drop. Dumbly he had wondered about Wolfgang on and off, had given him up for lost in the great world … but it was through Wolfgang's mother's knowing Stella's – Frau Stilz and Mrs Carroll at Baden-Baden perhaps – that she, Stella, albeit in the ten-year-old version, had one day taken his hand to enter a punt. Even then she had a brightness of her own, even then ... her glance had planted dormant seeds in him? which he, keen on keeping up with the crowd, had not noticed at the time? Himself as target for Cupid's arrows he would not contemplate, despite a liking for Philip Sidney, even in the privacy of his own head. He knows himself for all sorts of fool – Stella's formidable mother could at any time have updated the fortunes of Wolfgang. Apply to Mrs Carroll for further details, using, he thinks wryly, the appropriate military (except in her case civil) form.

He sees that he has always treated Mrs Carroll in the manner one approaches unused mortar shells. Returning to that day of months ago (as gone of course as the year 'Ought-three and their punting party), the Spring day when he had strolled down with Cutlass, when Bob Farley had shovelled winter out of the land drains, her 'false brightness' can be recategorised. 'None but the bold deserve the fair' – the tag is unplaceable but the thought stirs him. What could a girl of feeling have done in the presence of so ubiquitous a female parent? Not one to be upstaged, Mrs Carroll had also been taking the train, if in her case only as far as Birmingham. And Lawson the station master, a branch-line man himself, knew what connected to what and a man could wager she would have let out there were titles in the family. She would have seen to that, no doubt moving Birmingham as it were a good deal nearer in the process. Coincidence weaves fate ... Wolfgang's mother knowing Mrs Carroll ... Stella's getting to know his own sister ... Stella and Susan about the same age ... the families seated (Mrs Carroll much more amply so) eight miles apart.

It is the set of Stella's eyes doing him damage, no scholarly attention is required and no acquired wisdom can change it. Susan knows this, has known it long before the seeds had pushed up tiniest green into his consciousness. If Susan, why not Stella too – from her, or directly? Odd, how he has, come to think of it, never thought of it. 'Squad will ascend in columns of smoke!' One of the men's parade ground jokes. It had been a bit like that: Station Master Lawson's pretentious huffing and obsequious puffing turning to tank engine's steamy fuss; Stella carried off to Birmingham, to Aberdeen; he and Cutlass stopping a restful minute, Bob Farley declaring, 'I'd as lief step on um.' And then summer and then with harvest safely home heraldic beasts had got down from their shields, got up from their fields azure or gules and grunting, roaring, mewing, shrieking made a mad barnyard. Each week during this same time a letter had arrived from Stella to Susan and each week one had been carried back to Aberdeenshire. When he'd said, 'Give my kind regards when you next write her,' young sister had replied, 'Oh, I've been giving particularly kind ones from the beginning.'

Since June the Regiment had swallowed time quicker than the Bursar his famous oysters, though not quicker than now morning gulps the night. It amounted, his boldness through three months, to a couple of picture postcards. Salisbury and roses – and he'd thought twice about the roses. Messages in the space allowed had been next to nothing. Exactly a week ago they had spent a day on field security, examining a hundred of the men's cards and letters with that Oxonian staff officer – he tried out 'Oxymoron' but was unsure of the meaning. Seven days later he finds himself ashamed for the comments made by some of the others, effortless superiority, isn't that the ticket? The Socialists didn't bother with individuals – they accused by the yard, the barnyard full. Himself, he'd been struck not only by the brutally accurate comments of a lance-bombardier of the top intellectual class but by a lot of little things. If many spelt as they spoke, well … 'I'd as lief step on um.' He cannot remember one word of his own, neither at the back of Salisbury nor behind the roses, nor how he'd signed himself. Geoffrey Target is ashamed.

Today he is thirty-two, old by the standards of the camp. At two months Hostilities are in their babyhood and no one can say how long they would grow, nor into what. The older them, the shorter the lives of men. Such thoughts stand as a cliff and he feels strangely drawn to sleep in its shadow. In full day he drifts on the sweet shores of sleep, trying to moor there on a long rope. It's a blissful birthday spot to float amidst the changing reflections; these contain Stella's brow; Bob Farley's dark and bronze form cut out of hedgerow tapestry; and, rounded and gleaming like a dinner plate in one of the scullery sinks, a tableau from when he was nineteen – himself, Roger, Fenham, Stilz, someone else sitting about at college, in the Grove just by the river. They are watching the silent, eyeing moon as it rises – talking, trying to get Stilz's meerschaum pipes to light, talking. It is too far away, at the turn of the century, to hear what they are saying. Concerning the Social Question probably – Justice, Progress, Education. It had been easy then to paste long words six to a child's building block, to build up understandings of the world until they had to be cleared away at bedtime. But why that particular evening swimming in his head? … Irrevocably waking, Geoffrey glimpses through moonshine and meerschaum some unanswered question hanging in the boughs of the Grove with Bob Farley answering it.

Birthday or not … Sutcliffe's polite coughing, because you cannot tap on the flap of a tent.

'Come in!'

'Believe it's your birthday anniversary, sir. I left it as long as poss. Hope you don't mind the cha's in a mug.'

'Good man. Rain stopped?'

'Making up its mind, sir. Oh, RSM's asked when to parade the men and what you have in mind, sir.'

DITCHING

Geoffrey stretches out his last comfort. 'Been ditching. Ten ack-emma will do. Tell them we're digging trenches. Good idea if you're in a forward position. Done already over there – I was talking to a chap in the Mess the other night. Don't look like that, I know it will be wet and horrible. Unfortunately war doesn't get rained off.'

HER WINNING WAYS

NOVEMBER 1946

Of course there had been relief mixed in with the foreboding when Mrs Emily Shildon had proposed her home for the next and crucial meeting rather than the chilly Rural District Council Room behind the village hall. Neither Mrs Hilda Travis nor Mrs Marilyn Smout had needed to comment on the suggestion (typical Mrs Shildon), which anyhow had been immediately sealed by the Squadron Leader's enthusiastic 'Topping!'

And here they were walking up a drive instead of a garden path. Emily Shildon had explained the whereabouts of her abode, which they perfectly well knew already, by reference to the bus turn-round; she'd had the gall to describe her house as 'an awful old pile' and had excused its name of Parry Hall with one of her charming small laughs. Nothing could excuse the drive. 'It's a wonder,' said Hilda Travis, 'that they haven't put prefabs on all that grass.'

'I suppose,' Marilyn who was puffing replied, 'it might be pleasant in summer.'

'Hyde Park more likely.' Mrs Travis was given to the puzzling remark; Marilyn regarded her as clever and thought cleverness one of the more disturbing qualities which, if it had to exist, was better confined to men. November drizzled dankly over the scene, not quite enough for a brolly, but too much for comfort.

'Today should settle it.' Marilyn Smout wished she had more control over her sweet tooth or else that external circumstances had not conspired to feed it with food parcels still coming in from California, and the fact that she was still drawing Tom's sweet ration. But that was not the criminal-offence matter it might seem: like today's business it was an in-memory sort of thing, or had started as such – in memory of that wild and fiery, that *temporary* son who had stepped out of life nearly three years ago in 1944. Renewing his card … she could see that it had difficulties – and feel them in her overweight. But today was a day for drawing the line and for making a new start. Hilda apparently must have been thinking along similar lines. 'War's been over more than a year now, even in Japan.'

They turned a shrubby corner. Parry Hall, invisible even from the top deck of a pausing bus, stood before them. It was substantial and foursquare, its paint and glass shining brazenly in the dim November air. It had not once been requisitioned throughout the whole duration. There had been evacuees but only two as far as anyone knew, and the pick of the bunch at that. Both women had good working memories; hadn't it been said at the time that Mrs Shildon had stipulated horse-riding experience so as to avoid having anything too slummy living with her? They chortled grimly when Hilda said, 'I don't see any quadrupeds.'

The vicar's little car was parked outside and it was he who opened the door for them. He was still 'the new vicar', not yet thoroughly known – he was very well-preserved, everyone admitted it, but there were patches of vacancy in him which often emerged during sermons. A minute's silence even on Remembrance Sunday as in four days' time was quite a trial but it happened often on other Sundays. It was generally held that the new vicar was slowly embarrassing away the congregation. 'Are you soaked?' he asked.

'Damp but in good shape,' said Hilda.

'Oh, I can see that, Mrs Travis.' He sounded enthusiastic. Following her friend in, Marilyn Smout had the wild idea that he was referring to Hilda's figure which was trim and good at the expense of her own, but she prided herself in being a woman not easily undermined. She had never mooned over clergymen and could not understand it. She quite liked policemen but that was as far as it went.

The vicar's long hands reached for their coats. 'Nothing as simple as a hallstand I'm afraid,' he said, disappearing through a small door which had the word CLOAKS above it supported by a couple of absurd lions. It was all magnificently clean and there was a fire burning. A fire in the hall was so amazing that neither commented on it, though Marilyn steamed herself off a little.

'Wood!' The vicar was back – he was the sort of person who stands very still and then moves very quickly. They'd observed in church that he was a *darting* sort of man. 'She has it gathered up after the equinoctial storms. The Hall you know has much land acquired by one of Mrs Shildon's ancestors during the eighteenth century.'

'I suppose it's an acquired taste,' said Hilda Travis.

The vicar knew to laugh at jokes and had learned to recognise them but Marilyn treacherously wondered what she meant and if the remark was anything more than an expression of envy. For herself, she envied her neighbour's refrigerator which was not the same as covet. Parry Hall was too different to provoke any such feelings. She was impressed, and big enough to be impressed; it could be that Hilda was not big enough. It was a thought.

'Oh yes,' the vicar went on, 'her maiden name was Parry. Her grandfather was Sir Matthew Parry, the pig and duck breeder.'

'I see,' said Hilda.

'Not many people know she is a Parry – it must be one of the few things not widely known round here. It was through my being an amateur of local history ... local genealogy ... she does much voluntary work you know with the old people. That is why I am to convey her apologies for her not being quite here yet. Dear me, yes I have to phone the Squadron Leader who is picking her up. Do excuse. You have a nice fire to warm you behind and in front portraits to look at. That large one is the Hon. Mrs Emily Parry from the 1790s. She was known as *la Bella Signora* – great grandmother – the husband was on one of the Italian delegations. But, tell me, does she not strikingly resemble our own Mrs Shildon?' He darted off through another door.

'Well,' said Hilda, 'one lives and learns.'

'What was that he said about our behinds?'

'If it takes any notice of him, which I sometimes doubt, Heaven knows, Marilyn. And did you note "*our*" Mrs Shildon?' Hilda added.

'*Quite*. The Squadron Leader's Mrs Shildon more likely.'

'Very much more likely. He is picking her up; she will be filling him

18

up with her ideas – they will be sewing it up. One doesn't need second sight to know which side the clerical vote will be going.' Mrs Travis confronted *la Bella Signora* and pronounced, '"Hon. Mrs E. Parry – on loan to the National Gallery." We're in the National Gallery it seems.'

'That was the dispersal policy,' said Marilyn. 'All sorts of things went back to their owners.'

'Except for evacuees.'

'She is a handsome woman,' said Marilyn, being big. 'But resemblance, that's different.'

The portrait was almost full face. They looked her in the eye but it was serenely gazing elsewhere, possibly at the fire kept going by bits of the trees planted by Mr Parry or by her son to the benefit of their descendant – the windfall of centuries. Marilyn Smout said, 'They had to show a lot of chest in those days.'

Hilda produced a thin sniff. 'That's just the sort of thing Archie says.'

'*Did* he?'

'Probably still does. Archie Travis is not one for changing. "Immutable" is the best adjective, in polite company I mean. Immutable Archie.'

The exchange was almost being conducted through the third party whose serenity was touched with – if now untouched by – life.

'Oh I see,' said Marilyn. 'You mean … Up There?'

'I shouldn't say that Brighton was "up there", rather the opposite.'

'But "missing, presumed killed" though.'

'Missing all right. People may presume what they like. I'm sorry, dear,' – Hilda still seemed to be speaking to Mrs Parry – 'these things slip out sometimes.'

'Oh, I do understand.' Marilyn reached for her friend's hand but missed. Luckily the vicar had rematerialised.

He was full of his telephone call: they were on their way and Mrs Shildon had sent another message of apology. 'We shall be quorate and in the Blue Room. Elsie has the coffee there now.'

Elsie was one of the Barkers, every country place has such a family: large in number, seemingly indigent, probably indigenous – the first lot to have arrived and hacked a clearing in the forest. Such families have seen everything come and will be there to see it go. They have a careless ease about them. Elsie had maid's clothes on, the pinny if not the cap. 'Freezing day. Do you all take sugar?' She poured first for the vicar and then for Marilyn who missed out in refusing the addition (by spoon not fingers) of two lumps to her saucer. This lapse of resolve was possibly because she was engaged in suddenly recalling that this dark rosy girl of the type preferred in most operas with peasant dances – and was there an opera without? – had been in trouble with Americans long before anyone had seen a GI. Hilda was saying, 'Not for me, thank you.' 'Sweet enough without?' Elsie diverted the lumps to Marilyn's saucer, accompanying the action with a terrible louche wink. 'Madam won't be a jiff,' she said pleasantly and then left the room without any flounce. 'Elsie,' said the vicar. It was followed by nothing and most resembled 'Amen'. They sipped.

'I missed our last little meeting. I know that you ladies were at it. In a manner of speaking I missed the war you know. I was marooned in Toronto. Dear Mrs Shildon has filled me in but should we use the time to "recap"?'

Marilyn looked to Hilda who was stirring her sugarless coffee with a relentless scraping. Hilda spoke: 'Unlike some people, including the present incumbents, I was born in these parts and saw my father go off to the Great War and saw him come back. Mrs Smout knows my views. Our village did not do its duty twenty-five years ago and it has to be made good.'

'But how interesting!' shouted the vicar. 'You must mean the disbanded Remembrance Committee of 1919–1921. I have just completed a reading of their minutes. It got quite a way you know. It had chosen a design from Birmingham.'

'It had,' said Hilda. She delved in her shopping bag. Then spread before them was a plan, elevation or what-not of St George doing in a rather small dragon. The much-folded paper had seen better days but his long hands lifted it reverentially. 'How fascinating to see it, how fascinating! Birmingham right enough. But you must know why they disbanded?'

'Mr Roberts who kept the grocery was too mean to put a sixpence on the parish rate.'

'That did enter in earlier on,' said the vicar with a touch of professional diplomacy, 'but it was really because ... well, the two "candidates" ... they came back. They had somehow got left behind in France for a few years. It was a dramatic finale.'

'Makes no difference,' said Hilda. 'It was what my father wanted – Albert George Mason.'

'He *was* on the committee ... your father? Well, I never. In fact his was one of the last burials to be conducted by my predecessor.'

Hilda Travis was at her most formidable. 'What one war started, the other finished.'

'Pneumonia, wasn't it? My predecessor was a sound chronicler, a very model.'

'I have lost my son.' The words surprised even Marilyn who had uttered them. They were so simple, so absolute, so terrible that she was on the edge of tears. The vicar was on the edge of his seat extracting a handkerchief before she recovered herself.

'Tom Smout,' he said, 'yes indeed – *and* the late Mr Travis. Indeed, indeed. The wishes of the dead and the wishes of the living. Of course you must know Mrs Shildon's preferred option. It is one shared by the Squadron Leader. More modern in a way ... more *futurist*.'

'A bus-shelter!'

'A corner, Mrs Travis, a corner of Remembrance. A plaque, a sort of arbor, a seat and, yes, a shelter against the elements. She is thinking of the old people.'

'*Is* she? She is not by any chance thinking of the "poor man at her gate"? I am not having Albert George Mason, my father, ending up as a request stop.'

'This simply is distressing. He does not qualify. He cannot be commemorated in that particular way. Your late husband, yes indeed, the two Barkers, Tom Smout of course. Mrs Smout, did your son ... well, did he ever express any views about memorial matters?'

Marilyn knew only the truth would do. Tom had been so much trouble to them both, so often at the edges of crime that without all the help they had received from PC Witherspoon, the race between His Majesty's Prisons and the forces of the Crown might well have ended differently. Tom had always been so very much better at forgetting than remembering. It was so difficult, so confusing. Tears would not fall. 'He never cared much for pomp.'

Hilda crashed her cup, snatched up George and the dragon and crushed them into her shopping bag. 'I am leaving this house,' she said. 'She has got you all round her little fingers. I see it but that doesn't mean I have to stop and hear it. It will be a bus-stop and a bit of grass for the dogs to go on. It will not however contain the names Mason and Travis. It will be perfectly suitable after all.' She rose briskly. 'The two Barker boys. Tom Smout. *Sweet-papers!*'

REFLECTED GLORY

DECEMBER 1988

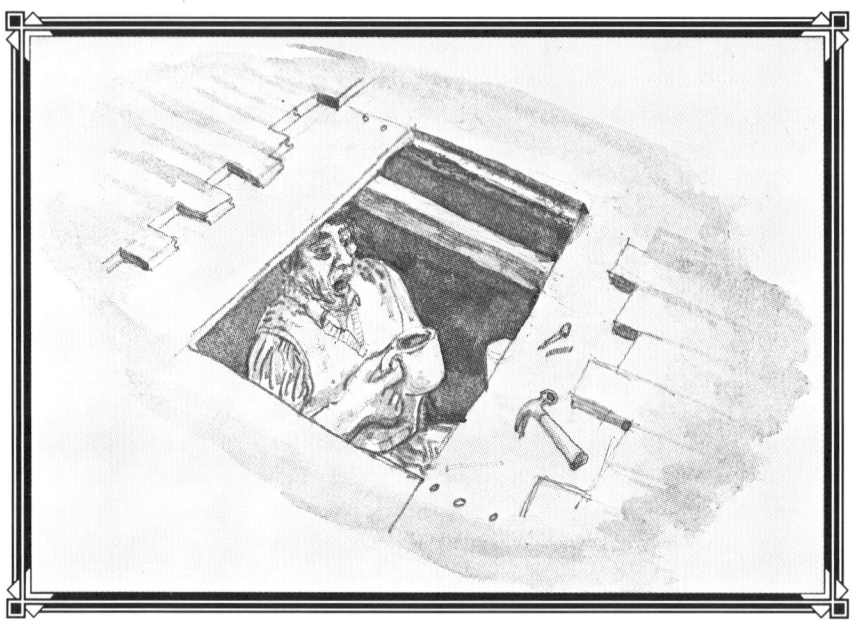

I've got to do something with my time ... See, write yourself down a sentence to get started and it stares you in the face. Then it's either stop dead or get on with it, which is what I want to do, not having anyone to talk to and it being Christmas Day. Sorry, no need for the fiddles and hankies.

In your forties like me, you start recalling bits of when you were a kid. One day my dad and me got on a bus to the Museum. Those days before the television age and before the idea of getting on became respectable, no one round our way went to a museum. One did though, my dad. You didn't get on in those days, you simply got *out* of the drudgery one way or another. It was just that most of his mates bunked down the rabbit hole of pints at the Club – holes twenty pints deep I mean, not the occasional jar. We must have seen hundreds of things that afternoon but what I remember is the bronze measures. He told me they were Roman but they were that well made they looked brand new. Imperial Standard they were and any citizen who felt bilked could take the stuff along and check it out. Stuck in my mind somehow.

I used to think writing didn't give you away – it might look like the proverbial inebriated arachnid or you might hold your ballpoint like a chisel – surprising how many do. It could always be typed, word-processed, set up in Baskerville or Gill sans serif. I'm not a man of letters though; I'm a Chippie, carpenter and joiner and – thinking back to that first sentence, I am a time-served man. Those bronze measures might help me to the point. You see, it's not just they were made by blokes who believed in the idea of them and knew bronze, not just that my dad took me – it's the kids. Not my lost son and his mother, I don't mean them: the kids at work. Imperial measure – feet and inches anyway – always intrigues them. They can be amazingly ignorant. 'Half-inching', you don't need to be time-served to know how stuff walks off sites and always has done, unless it gets a lift in a van; and you don't need A-levels to know about Cockney rhyming slang. But here was I explaining it all to Hawkey who's a lad from Clapham whereas me, if ever I get the bus home Birmingham way, it needs video and toilet for long distance. It's always a pleasure to see light dawn though. 'Half-inch' equals pinch, twelve inches to the foot. Maybe it does make me feel the hundred and five they think I am but the lot of them's been brought up metric on YTS. Imperial measure gets through to them the idea of a former world if only to brighten the toiling day with a little gleam like digging up Troy. Understanding, feeling a bit more alive.

By nature most folk are curious but they can't stick things together and so have to go making up fantastic explanations. Mind you, Education can often end as just like a filing cabinet with a place for everything and everything in its place. Me on my tod here, you'll just have to take my word that other people are interesting – interesting to me I mean. I shall go down the Bricklayers later on, but without much hopes of it. My Christmas all happened in a flash the day before yesterday.

It started out as what passes for a normal working day. You clock on between half seven and half eight – not clock on exactly because like a lot of firms now the Agency likes to keep things 'informal'. Two days ago we were all of us on the job by eight a.m. I need to set the scene for you which is rather an appropriate way of putting it. It's underneath an office block near the Brighton Road and when we first clapped eyes on it about three months ago it was just an empty cavern the size of a football pitch with about twenty foot of height to it – sorry, seven metres. We'd been told it was a big job. By New Year 1989 it had to become the biggest disco in South London. Some said two million was going in, some three, but I've heard five – pounds sterling. Introductions to the place were made by a foreman Paddy who then got moved on or out (you can never tell these days). He said: 'There's your canvas for you, blank it is but it's there you've to be putting in all the wishes of this perishing world.' Work, I've done enough of it, looking back. The first days were pretty bleak ones but the trade has been passed on into your hands even if it was obviously going to be the usual rushed bodge they pay us for. All I mean by that is that Ways of Doing Things is different from just getting things done. Catch me complaining, I keep my trap shut. My dad never got out of unskilled but *Made in England* was something he believed in – they all did once. He said Victory was the only thing badly made in England and that the War had turned things inside-out. Likely they just stayed that way. We got stuck in and three months later we had very near produced the brazier to take up all the combustible that's down here and warm … somebody's hands.

As I said, we had started early in the hope of knocking off by mid-afternoon. Christmas coming made it no season for all-hours and the ghoster squad. Come eleven ack-emma, we crashed out on the carpet rolls and surveyed the scene. Jock said, 'It's nae sae bad gif you look at it with your eyes shut.'

One thing pleasing to us originals was the good opinion of the special sparkies who'd been in. Each and every duct was in the right place and big enough. We'd had the painters around for weeks but they don't express a lot. The general opinion is that their brains die out in the fumes; mind you, as chippies we've been working with MDF, a sort of toxic but very workable stuff produced in the States but banned for use there. The special sparkies had left purring and told Hawkey all about how to work the strobes. The centrepiece was going to be this huge mirror with 112 angled surfaces. I'd cut most of the templates but the glass was now on, most of it. A real challenge all round, that was; it needed final fixing and like most things in this world it was temporarily hanging on a thread or bit of cable which Joker had christened 'Hawkey's Stanchion'. As we rested up on the carpet Hawkey was giving a bit of a go to the strobes, like God did when He'd delivered. Hawkey was entitled.

I should tell you – besides Jock and Hawkey and me, there's Tom, there's the Fielder and there's Joachim Coates. Half a dozen half-shattered blokes on heaps of half-price carpet. Like a lot of things it was supposed to have come off the boats, but I think that's been said since the Middle Ages and don't know how many boats we've got any more. Joachim or 'Joker' is a graduate and sometimes puts us right from reading a proper newspaper. We all get on together by now.

Hawkey put the lighting to normal and came back to join the heap. 'Sneak preview,' he said. 'You have to picture a thousand punters in the place.'

'A tenner to get in? Ten grand a night for starters.' Tom stuck out all his fingers.

'Not the stinking dosh,' said Hawkey. 'Picture the *talent*. Under them lights, know what I mean?' He spat into a pile of dust and chippings. In reality his name was Hawke and he'd been claiming on the Aussie PM ever since Joker told him; it was hawky by nature though, spitting for three months, always a tidy shot. 'They wear these white dresses,' he explained, 'and the blue kind of x-rays through to show everything underneath.'

Somehow this got through to the Fielder, which is not always the easiest thing to achieve. 'No one tell 'em?'

'It's intended on their part,' Joker explained.

'All their parts what matter.' Tom did a few gestures.

The Fielder was sitting next along on the heap and said quite a lot, for him. 'Don't work us, alright? I'll punch your head out.'

We fell to contemplating that hundred plus mirror; one of the few bits of sympathy I've got left for God Almighty is when he looked on his works and saw they were good. We'd slaved for that thing with Tom pulling muscles in his back previously unknown to him. The Fielder had sliced his thumb, standing gushing blood but no more talkative than usual until Joachim tore up his own shirt for a tourniquet – then he said thanks.

We were lolling at ease like I said when three blokes showed. Normal visitors scrabbled through what was fast becoming the Grand Entrance. This lot had keys. They had suits, three-piecers, and the portly one had his grandpa's watch chain on. They were scarcely older than my mates.

The chief one sniffed all points of the compass. 'The smell of the new,' he said. 'I am Roger Masters. Let me introduce my right-hand men, Charles Driffield here and J.N. Robson, IPFA, FRVA. With your skilled help, we rather hope to sew up the nightlife from Beckenham to Carshalton.' As this seemed mostly coming in my direction, I got to my feet. 'No,' he said, 'no, no.'

The man of letters with the gold ticker next said, 'They've earned a rest.'

'I know they have. Charles, do the honours.' What Roger Masters told them to do, they did it and one thing I know is that the weak give strong orders and the strong give weak ones. By now with the exception of the Fielder we were all at least heel-squatting and ready to get back on the job. All we'd ever seen of 'the other side' in months down here was Mr Wallis from the Agency to do the payout – Wednesday afternoons for some reason – him and someone to keep him right. These three had come from on high with gifts in cardboard boxes – looked like whisky and champagne and glasses to drink it from.

All three had quick eyes about them. 'Be a hell of a rush on the furnishing, won't it?'

'Boxing Day, Roger, no messing. It's Bateman's, need I say more?'

'They owe us, agreed. But, gentlemen, is there anything suitable for seating, sittable for suiting, eh?' This Roger's bigness had already got across with Jock bringing the best of our manky chairs and Joker dusting a couple of others centre stage. Checking my old horse for splinters, I sat on that. Eastern promise was set out gleaming before us. 'Bubbly's *Krug* and it's a single malt, Roger.'

'Christmas, Charles, when only the best does. Whilst you've been sawing and banging away, lads ... how shall I put it? We've been doing all sorts of less tangible stuff behind the scenes.'

'In fact,' said Charles, 'we were at a diplomatic reception only yesterday.'

'We were and I can report this exclusive fact, *viz*, worldwide they serve either fizz or malt. Had that from H.E. ... the ambassador from, where was it, J.N.?'

'Wogland somewhere,' said the man of letters.

'Exactly. These two beverages,' said Roger. 'No other choice. Not a can of lager to be seen.'

Jock was mumbling something about 'wee drams', his attempt to rise a bit to the occasion I suppose. Joker was looking more uneasy than anyone else I thought. Hawkey was working at not spitting; Tom bringing more chairs; the Fielder hadn't budged. By now the man of letters had a dozen big glasses line astern on Tom's pasting-out board. Tom had done a whole wall in seven metre drops and shown real talent for the work. These glasses were filling on the grand scale.

'Trebles all round!' Under this Roger's tousled charm you noticed his attention sniping, as if his blue eyes were gunbarrels – those Kalashnikovs. Just my feeling – he was a very pleasant-looking young fellow. 'Tell us a little about yourselves.'

'You've done a good job,' Charles added.

'As near as we were let.' Weeks back Jock had told us about YTS in

Glasgow, Social Skills from a bloke with a terrible stammer on him and transferred from Marine Engineering. He'd had us falling about but perhaps it had worked a bit. We were all too dug into pigging around to Radio One in our stye. Jock was making the effort. 'I ken fine that time's money but a piece of work has its ane needs.'

'The noo,' said Charles. 'The Spec was a work of art, take my word for it. Horses for courses is the name of the game. No one is going to bother with the quality of the woodwork. Be dark for a start. Hopping. State of the Art electronics ... What was that your Old Man was telling us the other day, Rodge? When you're poking the fire, you don't look at the mantelpiece.'

This comment I think did not best please Mr Masters and he turned on me. 'This work suit you, dad?' I explained that I had been apprenticed to the trade. 'Can be a waste of time these days. Consider how much time a man needs just in spending it, if he makes real amounts.'

I admit the whisky was beginning to oil us. Next I told him we'd been *averaging* eighty hours the past four weeks. Didn't necessarily go into every detail such as the ping-pong table nicked off a skip by Tom and then fixed by the Fielder. It was a big enough barn to keep some of its secrets safe from the three wise know-alls. They certainly believed in drinking from a wet glass; we were all perched there with malt whisky going down no slower than our normal copious tea.

But the Roger bird hadn't done with me yet. 'Bit heavy, wouldn't you say? Manual at your time of life.'

'My father used a shovel until he was sixty-five.'

This caused amusement among themselves; apparently they knew someone who needed following round by a man with a shovel. They had a knack of not quite sounding offensive. We were all wary all right but whisky doesn't watch out.

'Got a son yourself perhaps?' I explained that I had not seen him for four years. 'That's tough,' said Roger. 'He up North somewhere?'

'You might think it is.'

'You, what do you think? I don't have kids.'

'Not that he admits to,' said Charles.

'What's that supposed to bloody mean?' For a minute it looked on the cards they might fall out good and proper, but he turned back from it. 'I'm just concerned actually. I was wondering if he had followed on in the family manual tradition.'

'Followed his mother. Seen neither of them since 1984.'

The man of letters remarked, 'Hope you don't give the cow maintenance, old boy.'

'That's my business, I'd say.'

Of all of us it was Tom who had no head for drink. He turned over quick as that *Spirit of Free Enterprise.* We didn't stick together outside work but we'd seen it that time the lighting failed and we'd repaired to a local hostelry. Tom launched into speech. 'What's your game? You can tell me. What's your little game, like? SS, are you? I've seen it, straight up, no, hear me out.' The man of letters recharged his glass. 'Stoppages. Cheers! Don't get me wrong – I don't want stoppages. *Stoppages.* But it leaves you wide open, see?' Tom wagged a finger. 'Wide open.' There was the nearest thing to a blissful smile which his particular features could manage – and he took it with him when he fell off the chair.

'Good thing,' said Charles, loosening his tie, 'that we don't have the actual bloody hiring of skilled workmen.'

'Doesn't seem too skilled to me, that one.' Roger was pleasant.

'Wallpaper's a treat,' I said.

'You've had your turn. Now what about you?' He had picked out the Fielder.

'Ah'm not parlatic yet and not particular.' The Fielder held his glass outstretched for J.N. to fill.

'Good man. You must be from ... somewhere up there?'

'Ye'll not've heard where Ah'm from.' Somehow the Fielder was making it clear that, wherever it was, he was not going to bandy its name around before strangers. The Fielder is one of those blokes who say little, think less as far as you can tell but who move in a dark privacy, blokes who – against all the evidence – have a sort of weight. In his own time he'd accepted us as worth working with and he had fixed the ping-pong table. Things like that you value from the likes of the Fielder, though it's hard to say why. I could see Roger Masters saw it, whatever game he was on, as asked by poor Tom before his passing-out parade.

Maybe it was something they shared: people are surprising in a surprising number of ways. By now I was keeping my trap firm shut except to admit the water of life for which I was developing quite a taste. There was just Hawkey and Joker to go because this young Masters was like some inquisitor, and methodical. Could be he wanted maximum value for his money and this was his last chance. Inside a week or so us little band of brothers would be back in the four winds of making a living.

The mirror all this time was behind them and the facets made a sort of magnified background, bigger than life and sliced up. I was watching like a kid with a lolly on a stick.

Joker Coates was different from the rest with his degree in Philosophy. We'd had some quite considerable conversations. He lacks confidence though, Joker, and so it wasn't easy seeing how it would be. Hawkey, you knew would get passed over and in the lap of Joker it would all end up. He knew it. It was really odd how Masters and his henchmen had settled in front of us with all the whisky being pumped to conduct a Hearing or Judgement for that was what it had begun to look like. Joker may have thought he'd won the toss and chose to bowl. 'Very civil,' he said. 'My room mate in second year wanted to try for the FO. His father was Number Two in Copenhagen, so he'd been brought up diplomatically.' Despite the name, Joker was not given to jocularity except for the odd little pun which he would kind of sip at.

'Interesting,' said Roger. 'Varsity man, eh?'

'Came down this summer.'

'Don't blame you, exams are for suckers in my book. Never let it be said Varsity doesn't give a bit of gloss, mind you.'

Joker explained that he had stayed the course and collected a degree.

'Let me get hold of this. He's BA, BSc – am I right, Charles?'

'It's what the man's saying,' said Charles.

'It's what I'm hearing. Charles won't tell you but me, I'm just BF. From where I'm sitting though, where you're sitting looks like a very small pile of shit. Ach, it's Christmas so what the hell.' Roger stood up for the first time in ages. 'Time and the Greenhouse Effect, as they say. It's been nice, very instructive. Now we gotta wet this little disco baby's head.' He snapped his fingers and the man of letters, now obedient barman, gave into his hand and into Charles's a bottle of the champagne. 'You take one, J.N.,' said Roger. 'And one for Mr Bachelor of Piss-arts here. Come on, get set.'

On our rolls of carpet the little ragged audience of Tom (smile still perfectly fixed), Hawkey – spitless, the Fielder in his silence, me. Ranged in a row before us, the three smart suits and Joker, each armed with a bottle of the fizzy stuff. I was floating happy as a kid. Roger was supervising everything and he'd got them to loosen off the wire hold-fasts. 'Ease the cork a bit more than half-way and then give it ass with the flat of your hand.'

He'd done so well for himself, I think, through always knowing what he wanted and then getting others to do it. I can mind foremen of the real old sort who handled things a dream and always in their slightly special way. This though was going to be quite a little performance, a salute like what the RHA does for the Queen in Hyde Park on her Official Birthday.

'What goes up must come down' has always been one of our old trusty sayings. Flights of angels wasn't in it. It was the beginning and climax of the festivities all right. Roger had really got it together and all four corks took off as one. They must have hit Hawkey's Stanchion right on the critical point for it to give way like that.

It's quite a sight, a waterfall of mirrors, a hundred mirrors descending in a boiling rush. No one was hurt for a wonder. Dramatic, I'd say so. Expensive, Roger had something to say about that. Unrepeatable. One-off. Certainly.

This bit of reflected glory has kept me busy, if nothing else.

GETTING THROUGH

JANUARY 1967

Undeniably. Stuck. In the traffic. After all Mark's special avoiding action! It was one of those times for floating away felt Jane. *Repose* had been what her late grandmother had called it. 'I am dangerously short of repose ... ' It had been one of her grandmother's favourite words. Jane inwardly sighed in the direction of the bauble world of childhood when you had favourite word, best friend, special colour and one famous food fad. She glanced up at Mark's face with a notion of speaking of it to pass the time – childhood was a topic hardly touched on in their two years' (next month) marriage.

But the cliff of Mark's face did not encourage. There was a slight twitch there, a blood and nerve taximeter ticking with the disappointment of being stuck in the traffic. He had been so full of hope with that sudden shout of 'Gorton Street!', a long-lost friend, darting up it. Now he was stuck. Jane could imagine no way of scaling that cliff to carry up the balm of her feeling to him. Not analytical by mental temperament, Jane had subconsciously noted the dangers of a case where before long the baulked male might come out with something prefaced by the words, 'You might have ... '

Instead, she regards how neatly her gloved hands are cusping her knee and then looks out into the West End street, wondering how much it will have changed since Grandpa James's time; according to the old rogue his youth had been one long Mafeking Night and all the present talk about 'Swinging London' – that really got the old unrepentant going. There was no comparison! Grandpa's lifetime had voyaged through a solar system of different planets. Mark was deep into the changes happening now under the glitzy surface. There was someone called Chomsky – who he was, what he had written, she was unclear about that: his name was enough to be going on with, a real mouthful which most reminded her of the early morning bacon sandwich which she and Fiona and Glenys had chomped at the start of each waitressing day.

The opulent street was scruffy with litter when you studied it, left over from Christmas and the Sales, bits of fir tree on one shop and even a tasteful Santa – a ghost unplugged from his socket doing duty for Grandpa James. The West End at a standstill.

'What does he actually do, Percy Whatshisname?'

Mark grunted a sort of expectant animal noise and they were moving again. Jane let her mind wander round the notion of Mark the hunter; as if we poor humans at the hub of the new metropolitan world – new fabrics, new electronics all skyscraping away to the new tunes – connected back to us as we were in the jungle or digging holes for ourselves in cliffs. Mark, so silent, had been concentrating himself in the hunt for a way through, that rather than being moody and depressed – awaiting his chance with the traffic. You needed that patience to pounce. As well her question had come at the moment of move-off, for she ought to know what Perce does and probably could rake it up unaided. Perce and Zoe, there had been only a couple of meetings and hadn't there been, well, something rather *temporary* about Zoe? Perce was definite enough and not a person to overlook at six foot six or similar and with that red beard of his, all those cheerful shouts. Jane felt herself saved by the bell – or the toot of moving traffic.

Assumptions really – understandable – recognising people in the same light, in contexts. What lovers are supposed to have, a special light – only the aspects lovers recognise are everything. Normally, and Jane knows herself as a conscientious person even in musing, it is just aspects. There are the various tell-tale signs women recognise in each other and which men simply do not notice, such as periods missed or heavy, the skin surrounding the eyes. Ditto then with Perce, for Mark would exactly know the status of Perce in television, his contracts etc. After his long day Mark probably neither wants nor needs the accompaniment of bright wifely chatter.

And yet she then says, 'That's better, it's thinned out nicely. What I can never remember is the difference between Highgate and Hampstead but, wait a minute, I know Karl Marx is in Hampstead and Perce is in the other one – he told me once. I sort of mix them up, except I don't know how tall Marx was – there's only a bust and I really don't know the colour of his beard.'

Mark's long left arm comes out. It adjusts the air nozzle thing at her side and a tremulous snake of January air intertwines itself with Aunt Julie's necklace on her throat.

Perce and Zoe are a dinner party if they ever get there, Zoe for some reason supposed to be temporary – Perce then temporary for Zoe, if you put the same thing the other way round which you could, Jane thinks, after last night's lecture by Mark about equations. For a few seconds Jane in Majesty sits in judgement on Jane in Highgate (or Hampstead); they have stopped again but only for lights. This Jane, projected upwards onto the low ceiling of lit cloud, accuses the one in the car of unoriginal ordinariness. Not understanding algebra is an example. But Mark's way of explaining has always convinced, so the algebraic concept is a magic carpet. Don't stand outside failing to see what the first things mean: swallow it whole, scoot off, overtake gravity to juggle and swoop – because 'if b is always greater than c ... ' The nearest Jane gets to algebra is it must be like love, a world of its own.

Mark looks calmer now and that interesting word 'thoughtful' describes the settling of his face. He must be still pondering the problem of getting his ideas more widely disseminated. Maybe it is something in his brow which connects back to Sue and John's and all that eloquence he produced over the soup about new communications. He made it a flashing, writhing sea – electric eels, primary colours and not just because Sue's soup from Columbia had Tabasco in it. He had evoked the world everything was half into now and half held back from. John was jumpy about his new book which she could simply tell from the amount of radar Sue was putting out. John was much older of course and much more at risk from all the turbulence of the 1960s. Mark had said that books were gaols, the ideas in them locked from the light of day inside their pages. History, he had said, was made on the street and the street nowadays was 'a plasma of electrons'.

'This is bloody Hornsey nearly!' Mark carries out a sudden U-turn; there is still enough traffic to parp with surprise, fright, rage. That her husband is a good driver is one of the things Jane still believes about him and in more than two years of being a passenger – good or not – she has learned not to get implicated. Now at least he has done the right thing and they are bowling along with purpose. After her comments about Highgate and Hampstead the last thing Jane needs is another London H. Also she has learned to leave off her watch and wear instead the gold bracelet Mark once bought in France. An adjustment to her collar has deflected the cold air from her throat and Aunt Julie's necklace is warming nicely.

'Do we know if Zoe is still ... *around* with Perce?'

He seems to consider this but without coming to a conclusion. Why should he know anything of Perce's personal arrangements – Jane knows that he seldom approves of idle curiosity ... funny phrase. Still it would be helpful to know who the hostess was to be. Jane knows herself reasonably good at gatherings, good at avoiding the trouble which can arise from what her father – dear, antiquated thing – calls 'mucky manners'. Of course Mark does rather seek out the verbal variety as one who believes in total honesty and thinks of nearly everyone else as a hypocrite. For him life is an arena and already four people he was at Oxford with are in the Sunday papers. There were two last Sunday and she recalls the passion of his cry: 'David Howard *and* bloody Alex Lindley – *I don't believe this!*' Jane is sure that Mark's time will come and she is planning to obtain a book by Chomsky and to read it for a surprise. This evening Mark might be launched by Perce into the electronic soup. Perce could be as big in television as in real life, huge. One Sunday soon Mark will read his own name in the paper and it will be all right.

A big blowiness fills the outside night, echoing from low cloud which glows in saffron robes like the Hare Krishna people; urban lights preening the deep shines of theatre-going automobiles, all components of rare beauty almost in tune. Momentary relaxation, a scent of the evening to come descends on her. New people might be there, a possible future friend. Grandpa James, so good at stories and so almost good at not repeating them, sometimes has dipped into his oldest world, the Edwardian, to explain details of ancient etiquette. Jane seems to remember that it was Mark's red shirt worn with his dinner jacket which precipitated that account of exactly how the ladies withdrew to allow the men to take their port. Odd that even now in an evening the female component needed to put down the drudgery of pretence and have a talk. She savours it in prospect and hopes that during that meanwhile Perce will quietly fix Mark up. No denying that his looks would suit the screen and that his eloquence with an edge might flourish there. He could quite easily become part of the rage – Gramp's word and not quite suited to all this about being cool. Her husband, Jane gladly admits to herself, could quite easily fit exactly the style of the late Sixties, years which have seen so much and are quietly tiring of themselves.

His left hand parts from the wheel and she sees it coming, not to alight on her knee (it's some time since he has touched her much) which is her first thought, nor to adjust the nozzle thing which is her second. Instead, he fiddles with the tape-recorder 'cassette' which was so much bother to get installed. And it is Mark, clear as a bell, talking to them. 'Testing, testing. Ten, eight, six, four, two, zero … '

'Blast-off!' says Jane. It is so much like Cape Canaveral, now called after the dead President.

'When we consider what is happening today in the so-called "First World" we are – unknown to ourselves – operating a nexus of ambiguities. On the one hand for example are what I shall be referring to as our "functional mythologies"; on the other what we are tempted to think of as wealth-creating factories others have already designated as "the industrial/military complex". We are in danger of bringing simplistic perception to bear on wilfully obfuscated complexities. In the first respect we are as outmoded in our humanistic self-deception as in the second we are duped by deliberate misinformation. What is to be done? In order to see where we are, we must primarily cut through to what we are, and importantly what we are not. We are not free citizens of free countries speaking free speech and exercising freewill. These deceptions promulgate themselves within us, having been placed there by Classic Liberal Ideology, which will not admit itself ideological but instead offers us the delusion of individuality and shuts our eyes with notions of love, sapping both intellect and will with a century-old corrosive, branded *"Tolerance"* … '

SAINT VALENTINE ON TYNE

FEBRUARY 1990

Chances are you know the place if only from postcards or book illustrations. Where? The bridges of Newcastle upon Tyne. There's the big cantilevered span, scale model of the Sydney Harbour Bridge which local folklore insists was locally made and then taken over there in bits; there's the Stephenson high double-decker of wrought iron – local engineers puzzle how it still stays up. There are others. It's the height of their leap from the bluffs of Gateshead (largest mainline town between Newcastle and London) to the banktop of Newcastle itself which might have stuck in your head from pictures of the dramatic scene. Clearance for great ships was the idea when they built them but there's few alive now who saw those days.

One ship there is which has been part of the picture for several years, a superannuated ferry some tycoon runs as a night spot. There was a bit of bother over the question of rates and the vessel changed sides at least once. But no problem's insoluble with local councillors so well integrated into all aspects of communal life as they are up here. Why, it put the region on the national map for pace-setting twenty years ago or more – back in the Sixties.

Just back in the Eighties things began to happen down by the riverside. Don't let me push my luck, but you may also have seen photographic studies of the picturesque poverty we specialised in a century ago, all from this small area with its Dog Leap Stairs, Cushy Butterfield Ginnel, Baltic Chambers ... you'll know the sort of thing even without the pictures I cannot show you. These days a hundred years ago's no further than step inside a pub or boutique. Between then and now there's been a lot of nothing happening under the bridges; every year a few poor souls jump off one to keep the police launch busy. The population was shifted out into estates, the ships went to Rotterdam and daisies poked between the very cobbles where John Wesley had converted one afternoon hundreds of hungering Geordies to the celestial broon of Methodism. The siesta went on for decades.

It's fanciful to connect what began to happen next with the ship I've told you about, and as for historical parallels – handle with care! It's not so far, mind, downriver to Jarrow nor to imagine it as it was, amidst pasture and mudflat in the time of Cuthbert, Bede, the Irish and Saxon monks when they were the light of Northumbria, of Europe. Their little church can still be seen between pylons and storage tanks if you take the river trip. For them the first Viking longship to nose upstream, yes that was a spot of night and harbinger of Dark Ages. Migration, invasion, disease, they are all waterborne; new arrivals colonise the river banks – Jorvik, New York, Dubrovnic for all I know. Docklands. It is the ecology of invasions, preferred habitats. In no time at all money and concrete began to pour – piles were driven and people enough were driven by the idea of making a pile for the whole place to turn transformation corner. I've seen artists' impressions on posters which stretch the river into an aquamarine Amazon with watersporting executives darting out from their business parks. You can't be up and coming if you're too far from water: it's a not insignificant factor in the success we've suffered as a nation these past few years.

The trouble with showing anybody round is that you go into all the features. If you really know a place, whether it's your country, your town or your house up for sale, you start by being defensive when it comes to the bad points. A government scheme or estate agent simply brush them aside – holes in the floor can be 'features', and a pocket handkerchief lawn which every dog in a manner of speaking blows his/her nose on, 'mature grassland front and rear'. Real people rather like the shortcomings – they take longer to get to know and are more interesting. Holiday brochures never highlight the three hours' wait at Faro or Malaga but that's what next-door tells you about when it returns white-faced under the tan from the Costas.

Having done my bit, I invite you to forget the postcards and the generalities. I am going discreetly to leave the stage I have set. The final touches? Ice, not much, on the quayside cobbles, river going steady and black, bridges up there quite subtly lit I'd say. It's altogether a night to be inside with your TV and your cat.

She really is a girl in a hurry. 'Hi! I said to wait for me.' She measures her length in a terrible sprawling fall. One high and shiny shoe is twisted off and, between them, the old cobbles and new-formed ice have got her by the ankle. She gets into a sitting position and holds it. 'Damn, damn, dam... *nation*! I've only been here three days!'

The one and only bad thing about talking to yourself is having someone else in the audience. She has. It's a lad of about the same young age in soft and sensible and very silent shoes.

'You alright like?'

'Do I look all right?'

'Your hair's a bit messy but you do.'

'Very amusing. It's the Knightsbridge Casual and it probably's not come up here yet.'

'Be the only thing hasn't.'

'You tell me how you'd feel. I'm so ... so *bloody* annoyed. Why didn't they wait? You'd've thought they'd wait!'

The youth was squatting down and methodically retrieving her handbag and its badly scattered contents. 'Who's that then?'

'My party, stupid. Six of us went to the St Valentine's Ball. It's the nearest Saturday. It's all so horrendously stupid. I got stuck in the loo. They thought I'd gone. They didn't wait.'

'We call it "netty-fast".'

'I don't care the slightest bit what you call it. Ouch. Hang on – it's as clear as daylight!'

'Give us a white stick then.'

'Fiona made out to Jim that I'd gone off with Kevin. *Kevin*, I ask you! Jim believes anything he's told. Thanks.' She takes from him the restored handbag, fishes within and extracts one of the previously scattered items, a pre-war powder compact, quite a find in the Shepherds Bush market, to be found if at all up here in the possession of pre-war spinsters. But – instead of the face she mostly gets on with – the mirror gives her a small crazed-up version of the famous bridges. 'Everything's smashed!'

'You said it yourself,' he says. 'Saturday night.'

'What's that got to do with anything? I'm sorry, I don't happen to have my "Geordie" dictionary with me.'

'First thing you've said to me, that.'

'I've been talking to you for at least half an hour.'

He gathers up car keys. 'You never, man.'

'Ouch. I've knacked my ankle. Would you mind helping me up?'

'Be a pleasure. Canny does it.'

'Great. Don't let me detain you.'

'Nae problem.' Off he goes, careful-footed. She brushes at herself, sniffs. Off she does not go – the cobbles took a real mouthful. 'I say!' She knows he has heard. He keeps going. *'Please!'*

Slowly he turns, slowly returns. 'You'll be in need of what they've stopped off – "Temporary Supplementary Benefit".'

'I'm sorry I was rude to you, it didn't mean anything.'

'Howway.' Supporting her by both elbows, he steers her to sit on a convenient (and newly installed) bollard.

'What do they do about sprained ankles?'

'Shoot you if you're a horse.'

'That's not very funny.'

'Then feed you to the cat.'

'No, it isn't funny,' she says. 'It's not funny when one has a real live horse back home.'

'Me mam's got a cat.'

'I miss him.'

'He'd come in handy like with that ankle.'

'What name is it?'

'Adam.'

Suddenly she forgets all the awfulness and laughs, 'What a very odd name for a cat.'

'Na, I'm Adam, me. Mam was last surviving member of the Adam Faith fanclub. Cat's called all kinds. When Da used to look by, he called him "Willie Whitelaw" – which shows how long since. Our Maureen's tried "Sambo". Me, I don't call him owt specific. "Cat."'

'That is specific actually.'

'It's the nature of cats for names to drop off like water from a duck's backside. Not like a ship, that one.'

'I wonder where it's going?'

They contemplate just upriver on the other bank the Something-Princess lying moored under a hornpipe of dancing coloured lights.

'Nowhere. She's a nightclub – dance till dawn kinda style. Mebbes you'd not think I'd done me St John's. Your problem's contusion of blood vessels. Therapy's to encourage the blood supply back to the affected area.'

'My! How do they do that, Adam?'

'Hi-tech's use of ultrasonics to inhibit local coagulation.'

'What's lo-tech?'

'National Health's brisk manual application. If you divvent mind?' Adam squats before her and she feels the warm dexterity of his hands.

'Shall I take my stocking off?'

'Better not. Me granda had this thing about women's ankles.'

'*Did* he? Did he pass it on?'

'Not for a man to pass on, that. Nature brings fresh helpings. He passed on stories about his ships, except I was more fixed on the box in the corner at the time. Six years since he passed on himself. He'll be making for the Pole Star now.'

'It really is helping,' she says. 'Thanks. You wouldn't imagine the contrast. All this. No, don't stop.'

'Well, you're right there. Never been love lost between Gateshead and Newcastle. Father was from Wallsend and me mam's Felling. "Witsend" she said for her home address. He worn't all bad – more weak. Went down south.'

'Most of my friends are in that club – parents split up.'

'Never stuck except the twice – me and our Maureen. No, he went south just about the time me mam's da went west. He was a soul good both inside and out. Me father was more the missing link. One thing I remember he said. "How can you tell a Gateshead police car?"'

'I say, I say, I say. You can't tell it anything ... I don't know. Give up.'

'It's fitted with a roof-rack.'

'I didn't mean Gateshead, I meant the contrast up here and where I come from. You're like all males – you never listen, just interrupt. The difference across this river's infinitesimal. Thanks, I'm all right now.' But you can't rush ankles and she soon has to say, 'Oh dear. You couldn't help me upstairs to my place, could you?'

Her place is in what used to be a warehouse for storing return coastal cargoes. In its time it had housed everything except the coal you didn't take to Newcastle though you might have to soon. Now more literally it housed southern imports in sixteen smart apartments. Hers is right on the top floor but Adam is really good at helping her up all the stairs. It's penthouse style with striking views – of Gateshead. He's impressed. Sitting him where he can look out, she plummets into the Habitat settee. He puts her feet up, neatly loosens straps, removes her treacherous shoes. She is told to wiggle her toes. He sits handsome and moody and tells her, confessionally almost, that he has worked in London but does not feel he knows the south.

'Well,' she says, 'where would I begin? Somehow – but that's not it either – they don't believe in anything.'

'They have to believe in something, man.'

'And you, what do you believe in, *Adam man*?'

'I believe I'm here,' he says – and she finds a sort of cheer in it.

'And as for parents, they have a whole *set* of beliefs, dozens. It's like a honeycomb with all the bees gone out.'

'Happens to oldies.'

'I do love them,' she says, 'and they've always looked after me.'

'I see that.'

'What *can* you mean?' Surprisingly, this Adam can be surprising. Then there is the warm fact of him and there is his unknownness.

'The way you conduct yourself.'

A topic to change. 'Buckinghamshire is so different. The stars are the same though. It's not such a big planet.'

'Is as well,' he says.

'Look around – Daddy's invested in me. He found me a bit of a job till autumn, this apartment, the car … Then I repay it by studying at university.'

'You're canny enough.'

'Just look at it though. Johanna can't credit it – a lifetime's consumer durables. Half the stuff's not unpacked. I fixed the coffee machine first and it's all set – *and* in reach. Does he take sugar?'

'Beg pardon? I was miles away.'

'Gateshead this time or just the Pole Star?'

'Two please, the normal.'

MONTHS

'Not in Berks, Bucks and Oxon it isn't. Sugar's practically banned from the table.'

'*Way*-ae!'

'You tell me how you'd feel spraining your ankle on your first Saturday night in the heathen north. What do they do here anyway, besides swilling?'

'Same as anywhere else. fillums. Some go to Midnight Mass.'

'You're not a Catholic?'

'Don't even support United, me. What's that you're fiddling on with?'

'EXECUPHONE,' she says. 'Every day something comes TNT. Daddy's gone over the top with this. Not connected though.'

'It's cordless.'

'Still have to connect them. It says here. And it says its number on these little cards. Go on, take one. It's just that you're the first to give it to, that's all.'

Who can tell what is saved by the bell? They both jump, Adam more so.

'Damn,' she says, 'damn. That's Johanna back. She *always* forgets her key. Still, her rent's the only return Daddy's getting on his investment.'

'I'll be gannin. She can drink me coffee for me.'

'Don't be so jumpy. All right. I'll say you were the man from TNT. And you've been a brick.'

'Give us a card then.'

'And you give me a ring when I'm connected.'

'And you keep them toes going.'

'And you let in Johanna. Keep that card until I'm connected.'

'Nivver lost a thing yet, hinny.' And out goes Adam on his two good feet.

THIS SIDE OF EASTER

MARCH 1956

At last we alighted at the Gare du Nord ready to breathe our first Parisian air. Immediately we were surrounded by portering staff of all shapes and sizes but with the single purpose of seizing our few pieces of luggage – and this when I could easily have carried all, thus freeing May to cope with considerable documentation in a frame of mind to meet an officialdom of which we had experienced more than one example on French soil. Three porters had finally attached our belongings and we followed them miserably along the *quai*. Truth to tell, they were an amusing trio, the smallest staggering with May's case which contained clothing for all seasons, the middling one my modest valise, and he who must have originated within a giant equatorial African tribe the briefcase from which I am rarely parted at work or play.

Should I explain a lack of decisive action on my part? As a child May had been in France on no fleeting visit but for over a year. She claimed early memories of the skies of the Loire, the feeding of assorted French cockerels and hens, the diurnal sound of the French tongue. In thirty years of marriage one cannot learn but to defer to many things and in particular the living myths of one's spouse's formative years. The Campbells had fled the day before the Kaiser's waves of field grey broke upon Belgium. That was May's fifth birthday. In short she has maintained a copyright on the 'Auld Alliance'. Secondly the termini of a great city are overbearing. The Roman god Terminus is not one I have seen depicted but I hazard an expression of divine uncertainty, the very feelings we experienced in approaching the barrier.

Getting our belongings out of French hands loomed large, I must admit. We had foreseen that the Collector of Tickets would sport braided finery the equivalent of – shall we say? – a colonel of the Argyll and Sutherland compared to the lowland status of the men at Calais and Amiens and the later person on the train. She was putting together French and it does not shame me to tell you my heart was beginning to bleed. She had opened with a strongly whispered *'Messieurs, s'il-vous-plaît ... '* when in a waft of doffed fedora a stranger took charge. One extraordinary second later he had repossessed us of the paraphernalia, unclicked my briefcase to expedite formalities and danced us breathless to a table under the window. There a *garçon* fussed up coffee, mineral water and things between biscuit and cake.

'*Tiens*, you have without doubt voyaged too many hours for comfort. I am Marcel and I must how do you do?'

His charm, abstracted at a distance, might leave cold the British temper, but near-to it was striking and genuine. My wife May whose sang-froid and savoir-faire rarely fail her in her native tongue (English as spoken in the unpretentious end of Morningside) said: 'How unexpected and how very welcome!'

'It is the smallest I could be able to do to you.'

'It is very civil of you, sir.' May looked at me in sudden inquest but guessed, I think as quickly as I did myself, that it derived from Boswell whom I had been reading on the journey. The past is a foreign country, and it served well enough. Our new acquaintance bobbed a sitting bow and said simply enough: 'I have not forgotten the War.'

It cannot be denied that this was pleasing. The memories of wrongs done by nation to nation tend far to outlast residual gratitude between the nationalities. 'There are, you know,' our new friend continued, peering behind him as he spoke, 'other people. *Agents de l'état, peut-être ...* who do not share our views.' He was a romantic personage and his smile the very sort of article which is insured heavily in California. I would have wagered that my wife is a woman not easily charmed, but his smile was to be of some importance in domiciling her, so to say, after forty years once more in France.

'*Vous êtes trop gentil,*' said May.

'But this is absurd!' He circled the air in Gallic flourish. 'We know only the one another in code. *Comment t'apelles-tu, Madame?*'

So introductions were effected and we became Marcel, May and 'Al' (for she has so contracted my name which is Albert). It could be said that we became Marcel, May *et al* – for the conversation turned exclusively French between them. Its drift seemed to concern the (to them) fascinatingly springtime nature of the female appelation: April, May and June. Having little to contribute, for myself I observed the scene passing beyond the window, for example the strange buses with rear verandas known to us from visits together to the Arts Cinema off Princes Street, occasions which had endowed us then with a raciness I found wanting in the Gaulloise-scented air. We had travelled hopefully enough, but we had arrived not quite how I had pictured it – in the comradeship of travel. Thomas Cook & Son, with whom we had booked at a very favourable tariff available to those reserving 'this side of Easter', had provided both streetplan of Paris and a bewildering guide to the bus routes. We had resolved on the easier alternative of the *Métro* whose hooting doors we knew from films. Now Marcel had taken charge. He and my wife had made, it seemed, arrangements involving his car and a restaurant.

It was perhaps that our arrival, despite its aura of salvation, had landed on the wrong foot. Some matters go uneasily into the publicity of the written word and I say this as one whose father had passed on a respect for Literature and Philosophy – the flower of Edinburgh's Eighteenth Century wafting down the generations. Throughout the Great War my male parent had shouldered the burden of the Commission for Civil Supply; my earlier days saw important comings and goings to our house. In those significant days nearly all things were to be measured in terms of their *Consequence*. People's feelings and affections existed quite unspokenly. In our many years of marriage May and I had not been abroad and the business of finding the hotel (a thing of no consequence in itself) would have signified a mutual achievement. Marcel's advent had thus forestalled plans in the making since Amiens. The very question of settling for the partaken refreshment did not arise. It had been taken care of, which was somehow suggestive of the encounter's having been pre-arranged.

I was jealous of him. It was as distinctive and I confess undermining as the world beyond the window sweeping along with all its alien consequence. From my parents I had learnt that self-esteem is a component of civic virtue and for my wife to shine has always given pleasure. If there is a wee mite of the proprietorial in that, it is not necessarily culpable. We are all 'at sea on dry land' – I hear Father saying it – the ones we live closest with can be surprising – and so they should indeed! It was simply that in Marcel's company May was becoming a person I had never known. In no time at all switches bring into question all that had previously been assumed and are deeply of consequence in what must follow. Jealousy always quavers at dimensions unknown and is not merely the littleness of ownership. I was in that land as well as in Paris but the inner landmarks had no illustrated catalogue from Messrs Thomas Cook.

His car was low-slung, black. Climbing into a rear seat, I kept firm hold of my briefcase. Street after grand street passed by, but airless to my thought and lacking the blowy grandeur of our New Town at home. It was a city picking itself up from nothing more severe than the shame of enemy occupation and it was taking long enough about it. Soon I recognised the Sacré Coeur looking for all the world like a whited sepulchre. Scruple reminded me that God is in the hands of human aspiration and that His decent *pieds-à-terre* in Scotland are but such an expression of the upward-looking earth as this. I retained sufficient recall of the streetplan from which I had been parted by Marcel and my wife to know we had reached Montmartre. We stopped at our hotel, by name l'Etoile, and I was reaching for the handle when May said – our driver having athletically left the vehicle: 'He's seeing to the porter.'

I am afraid that I replied, 'He is good at that.'

'What is that supposed to mean?'

'Only that this is *our* hotel, *our* luggage and *our* holiday.'

'I cannot think,' she said, 'that we need go into our luggage before lunch.'

My ear was astounded, our having been on the move for almost the rotation of the earth. 'We need to see the room!'

'Marcel knows the place, Albert dear, and he said the rooms were perfectly adequate. Besides, I don't see what we could do if it isn't. And if it isn't,' she added with a flourish of what my father used fondly to call feminine logic, 'the less time we spend in it, the better.'

A working life in Banking places one where two kinds of judgement need applied: of the account and of the holder of the account – 'credit-worthiness' is the modern term. They are there because they want of you; you judge the risk and what lies on the table between. Liking or its opposite must remain at arm's length. In the back seat of Marcel's car I summoned this training to my aid. If it was money, he was going a far way about it; if not, what? The puzzling of the mental faculty was restorative. Had my companion been not May but the beautiful imagined daughter perhaps ... Marcel being Gallic ... but even that would smack more of Daphne du Maurier than the Paris of 1956.

You will know it is a long time since Scotsmen have thought of censoring the reading of their womenfolk, longer since they did it. May and myself have ever respected each other's tastes and watched lest the domestic tyrannies developed. One does however observe the bedside reading of one's spouse and I had remained amused by her predeliction for romantic novels – of the better sort, let me add. That field of fiction has never drawn my attention. Bedside tables gather their own detritus and on mine, slowly devoured or finally abandoned, linger tales of detection and espionage: a banker's holiday when I came to consider the matter. As deliberate policy I made myself to be calm and utter no comment even when a uniformed flunky carried our cases from the boot of the car. I was in possession both of my briefcase and myself.

Whatever our French friend was engaged in took a length of time during which May silently occupied herself with the prinking allowable to women, swivelling the rear-view mirror and then returning it to approximately the original angle. Tiredness sometimes crystallises into meditative composure. My mind had now settled into John Buchan lines and was revisiting the lower slopes of the Leith & Portobello Commercial Union case when I had saved my bank nearly half a million sterling. On vacation I was recapturing vocation, the truest spring of a man's self-confidence. The silence between May and myself had grown into a thing more of mutual puzzlement than hostility; illustrative indeed of most adages respecting the leaving of one's native land.

Marcel returned with routinely charming apologies. I began to feel I had some measure of the situation. Rarely had I been so consciously analytical in temper. 'Had you a place in mind for luncheon?' I enquired.

'*Bien sûr*, if you are *d'accord*. It is in Vincennes where we are to pick up the big contact.'

We took off like an aeroplane and 'my companions' were flowing entirely as I could make out in French. May was a dozen times more fluent than I had suspected was in her; but then I had never had much occasion to know. In the distant days when she would fancy herself pregnant each summer there had been French courses at that place near St Andrew's Kirk and no doubt the odd WEA class. It is possible a childhood ear takes in a pattern – the 'loom of language', don't they say? Observing the nape of her neck and flashing slices of face served me by the wrongly angled mirror ... surprise brimmed over my new-gained resolve. Here was more animation than I had seen in twenty years! Speaking a foreign tongue, do we diverge into alternative possible selves? Our good Scots tongue of course has its own luggage to bear.

The town or suburb of Vincennes is at some distance from Paris. I knew of a partly ruined castle and also that Napoleon in the power politics of the day had ordered a ducal execution there. It was a suitable destination for the present business perhaps. And, as at the station and hotel, things were to appear as if pre-arranged. Marcel drew up at a restaurant in a sort of public park. Its buildings of wood and wrought iron were old and unpretentious. It must have been the Proprietor himself who met us and conducted us to a table by the window; the place was kith to a conservatory. It came as no surprise to find one already seated there – 'the big contact'. His appearance suggested parts of Europe which Messrs Thomas Cook in their revival of pre-war touring had not selected to advertise this side of Easter. His spectacles were of strange and heavy design, as was he – in his build I mean. Even abroad he had a most foreign look. Marcel introduced the man as Squirrel whereupon he lumbered upright to bow to May and then to shake my hand across the table. Banking teaches a man to look a man in the eye and there to register the uppermost attribute. Squirrel's was guarded watchfulness.

You will know the ordering of food is a most serious affair in France. Some collusion between Marcel and my wife resulted in her recommending certain dishes. I must say that I did not feel biddable in the matter and in as neutral a tone as I could muster opted for my own choice of onion soup to be followed by rabbit. The menu gave this as *lapin au moutarde*. It happens that I use English after the Scottish manner and the word 'rabbit' is one a Scot can bite into. It sounded with particular clarity and was to prove a culinary preference of more consequence than any amount of idle French chatter about stomach and table – however unexpectedly fluent. Immediately I was aware of a change in Marcel's attitude towards *et al*. Looking closely at me, he said, 'But that is exactly ... the *mot juste*, "monsieur R".'

'Sometimes we must ... eat our names.'

'Precisely. Always in fact. Perhaps it is fortunate that we do not have *l'écureuil* for choice today.'

This exchange surprised May more profoundly than her linguistic flowering had amazed myself. She was nonplussed. The third man's small smile simply lit up how grim a one he was. Care was required but having chosen to grasp the nettle danger I must not lose nerve. The new respect was evident still in Marcel's referral to me over the *carte des vins*. Looking in his charming, unsafe face, I said, 'They have numbers, why do you ask?'

'Fourteen?'

'Fifteen,' I said. 'There have been changes.'

'That is good.'

'People have talked,' I said, sensing a fullness in my lucky strike. Eating in France demands a quite unreasonable discussion of the comestibles which in turn swallows the attention of the eaters. When May had made a partial recovery from my seeming lapse into inanity she exchanged a few such words with Marcel albeit listlessly. The food was excellent but there was something heavy upon us, a Cold War chill perhaps. Marcel had become circumspect and at his own wedding Squirrel would not have been expansive.

A sweet course and then the coffee had arrived before Marcel returned to his purpose. 'You go to … *that city* on Thursday?'

'Before then,' I replied. 'That does not concern you.'

He accepted the slight rebuke and addressed Squirrel in some unidentified language. A small packet resulted which was handed across the cloth to be placed by me in my briefcase.

'You must remain here,' I said, 'for perhaps one half-hour. We return to Paris by taxi.' I had noticed a rank at no distance from the park gates. I shook their hands and took May's arm.

The taxi proved expensive but the people at l'Etoile were no trouble when we moved out; it was as if they had expected it. In the end I think I may say that our short stay in the French capital gained a definite edge from the presence of that dangerous but unopened packet in a socks drawer at our new hotel. Keeping a sharp eye out for faces and cars, we were almost like lovers in a film.

I finally disposed of Squirrel's gift in a street waste bucket belonging to the City of Edinburgh Corporation. It has always been a town – at least during my lifetime – specialising in safety.

MIXED DOUBLES

APRIL 1928

If you cut up by the new tennis courts through the increasingly tamed wilderness of Hanging Wood you could get from the Feathers and the streamside houses to the village in record time. It was steeper than the road but so much more direct. People had simply made it by forging chest-high through the ferns last year after the courts had been put in. The Rural District Council – run, like so many things these days by a 'colonel', the go-getting P.R. Hallet – had been shrewd enough to adopt this people's path, even to the extent of edging and tarmacadam. Locals of the Doomsday sort shook their heads. Hallet was not truly local and was rumoured to build bungalows on spec.

For residents less stuck in ancient mud the new 'walkway' together with the courts added up to quite a bit for modernity, for a rural spot. Things were stirring forward now in 1928 and not just in the leaf, the anemones, the welling variety out of rich woodland earth; but also in a sense of returning future. Colonel Hallet had got in men from Chelmsford. Their steam lorry tucked in neatly for its size by the Feathers, they had laboured for three days doing the path and not merely with pick and shovel but with a petrol-driven stamper. During daylight hours your hearing trembled (more for some than others) to the faint *crump-crump-crump* from the heart of Hanging Wood.

But now it was Sunday. The men had just knocked off and were watering themselves and their steamer before the long haul back to Chelmsford. Now there were voices in the wood, light, young and in keeping. New leaves spread themselves and glowed. Nothing was not translucent on such a day.

'Roland's got the key, Mo.'

'Who's got the balls?'

The merest titter danced across from one to the other, nipped in the bud by Rose with an *'Erhum'* which said everything – about daring and parents and recognition that Mo's perfectly innocent remark had formed a little booby trap. There was no feeling of being boobies. Rose took the other girl's arm.

'I'm a duffer at tennis, but don't tell anyone. Roland, I hear, is tolerably superb.'

'At everything,' said Mo, 'is the general opinion.'

'Not necessarily the *colonel* opinion though.' Rose put a braking pressure on her younger cousin's rounded arm. 'Young males and motor cars should be kept apart. Coo-ee!'

'Coming.' It was George's voice.

'Hallet minor taking the lead for once.'

'There *is* something,' said Mo thoughtfully, *'something*. But search me what it is.'

'It's called "intuition" and introverts specialise in it.'

'I'm not that much of an introvert.'

'Mo dear, there's nothing terribly wrong with being an introvert. Men may think they prefer more showy types like me but since when did men know anything at all?'

'Or what they know,' said Mo, 'is not particularly knowable.'

'One can be too deep for one's own good, cousin mine. The sun's shining, God's in his heaven and all that. *Now* what's keeping them?' The girls had reached the tennis court gate and its bars and wires gleamed black and pleasing as a new bicycle. 'It's not *what*, but who you know,'

Rose continued. 'And the sons of the RDC have certain advantages. If, instead of being the blameless maiden I undoubtedly am, well ... I might say that our colonel has seen himself well set up in the contracting line on the rates. Not cross my mind, Mo dear, were it not your beloved Uncle John, my dearest pa, has become a wee bit cynical in his old age.'

'Daddy would have been forty-five yesterday. You must know he was killed on his thirty-fifth birthday. Ten years!'

'Uncle Trevor's still too difficult for dad to discuss really.'

'He's with me you know,' said Mo. 'Fixed. No old age for him to get cynical in. He taught me tennis on his last leave. He said if I kept at it I'd break his service.'

'Did you? I mean – keep at it?'

'You do you know.' Mo had picked bluebells and was plaiting them into a sort of coronet. So intent, dark, busy. Rose thought dutifully of Uncle Trevor. Ten years was a long time, except for being dead in. She could remember only her old extinct pangs of jealousy, for Maureen had been as beautiful then as now – steady in that as in everything. Ten years ago was bang in the middle of that awful patch of too much tooth, huge elbows and knees, ridiculous hair. Now at twenty-four Rose was well-grown and could approve her image in the glass. And if, three years younger, Mo was still the true stunner, well today's fashions probably suited her own looks better. They'd landed nothing much as yet but Rose was fairly confident they'd have the required breaking-strain if the sea ever came up with a suitable fish.

George had at last arrived with three racquets awkwardly akimbo under one arm. Famous for Classics and brains, he had surprised Rose's mother recently by confiding in the post office a change of educational plan through wishing to be a surgeon. He was even prepared to go to the lengths of Edinburgh to see it through. His management of the racquets did not inspire huge repose at the prospective delving in people's interiors. Rose had noted that there were those who thought only in terms of the material world, their brains clambering about in it, happy as monkeys. George, she could tell, gave it no thought at all. It was little short of a wonder each morning that his shoes found themselves on his feet.

George said, 'Roland's gone back for the other one.'

'I was thinking perhaps he'd give a handicap by playing bare-handed!'

'He's not as good as he thinks himself, not by a long chalk.' George applied the key to the shiny black gate and it hurt Rose to see it.

'Let me,' she said after a bit. It was a hard court, the very latest thing, and Colonel Hallet had contracted himself to do it in asphalt or something which was supposed to come from the West Indies by ship to the Port of London. Rose hadn't yet made up her mind on how different the places of the world might be, or how much the same. At twenty-four it was getting time to find out. Apart from the dances at the Golden Lion which were getting thin, there was one word for what happened at home: *nothing*.

Greenish lichen had begun to move onto the court; Hanging Wood investigating. Mo had picked up a stick on the way and was using it to write or draw on the ground. George was showing no sign of mental activity and Roland seemed permanently absent. Rose watched the end of the stick. Mo had written WHY, added a question-mark, scuffed it all out with her shoe. Mo did nothing for effect as far as Rose could tell and so it was another small mystery.

'How is Mr Starmer?' George was gearing himself up into manners.

'Dad's the same old grump.'

'My parents aren't speaking.'

'Literally?' Mo had wandered up in support of this outbreak of gentilities.

'Literally and in every other way,' said George. 'He's the usual thing, drink and all that. He *was* a colonel by the way, acting – for about ten minutes in some carnage or other. People say he wasn't. Half the courtesy ranks now it's getting respectable again, people invent them.'

Rose said: 'He's better known than most and he does more before breakfast than I do in a week.'

'My Aunt Margaret,' said Mo, 'was saying that you wanted to be a surgeon.'

'It's not so much want as need. The cultural thing is dead,' said George. 'After Tennyson, not even a possibility and politics – my God! – what are they nowadays?'

'Boredom and wireless communiqués,' said Rose.

'So you must see there's no help for it but something ... uncontaminated. Cutting someone open gets you ... inside.'

'Obviously, dear boy.' Rose was amused – at least he'd got hold of the basic idea.

'The human body, it's *uncontaminated* because it's not man's fidgety doing. It's the Temple, even if defiled.'

Regarding the others, Rose was struck by them as a pair. George who had gone off in such unexpected fashion was in tension and Mo curved to it questing, a bit like her scratched question-mark.

Turning her back on these spare bits of punctuation, Rose walked to the other end of the court. Thank Heaven for cigarettes! Without them not only would the West End theatre be stuck for business, but neither might she so easily detach herself, chaperoned only by a little black cat on a red packet. Except she was too old now to require chaperonage – except the whole idea of it was going, or had gone. Pluming the smoke of Craven A as delicately into the April sun as all the trees' glowing renewals, Rose was in translucency and saw how the generations were cemented together in shared memory – laid down if more like asphalt perhaps than burgundies, like poor Uncle Trevor ... stratified. It was terrifying. This was you now – you looking out through shiny mesh at the standing wonderment of what air and minerals had raised up. It was the coming-out dance of the natural season with all the grace and beauty the tawdry social counterpart intended but with none of the horrible shortcomings so marring things for the Hon Cynthia Fuller, the only debutante known to Rose. Poor Cynthia had only escaped the worst through her chaperone's having taken a fit.

Tennis preparations were totally stuck for want of Roland. George and Mo had run out of words or inclination and were mooning about at the far end – happily enough perhaps. Outside, Life was more active and looking in, life was embodied in a squirrel not of the little auburn kind but one of the grey American imports. He had just as much awareness of her – humans in a cage and squirrel outside, his little head and ears in an aura of hairy brightness.

'Hullo,' said Rose most softly. The ears twitched and he seemed to accept the greeting. 'Hullo, little thing.'

Agile and hairspring, he was off. In a trice at the base of a tall tree. Then – a pause of stillness between everything he did – up it, hands and feet hauling it in. The bullet pinned him and the gunshot sound carried on through the woods to find itself an echo somewhere down by the stream. He fell back to the root, leaving a blotch of his blood on the gleaming bark.

Roland appeared.

'Not bad at all, eh? The old eye hasn't lost its cunning and the three-eight's handy as ever was.'

'How could you?'

'Sorry, Rose. Did I startle you?'

'You killed. You killed a harmless creature.'

'Not so much of the harmless. They're officially vermin, you know, and they're driving out the little red chaps who are as British as you and me.'

'That makes it all hunky-dory, does it?'

'I'm truly sorry if I startled you.' They were now within a few yards of each other, the netting between.

'Well, you didn't in the least.' Rose went to join the others. It was scarcely believable! It was worse because at twenty-eight Roland was just enough older, further down the stream so to say ...

'Here you are, young shaver! Mater's old bat to make up doubles. Together with iron rations.' Roland extracted from the small army pack he had with him a few apples, chocolate bars and four bottles of pop. He dropped it with a clump to the ground. 'Enough to feed a battalion.' Roland wound up the sagging net. 'Bring us a racquet, will you, Rose?' She did so and he measured the height, made adjustments. 'Do you forgive me?'

'It was just terrible.'

'It was a "varmint".'

'You're not sorry at all.'

'Come off it, Rose, when I said I was, you said I wasn't.'

'It's of no importance.'

'I suppose not, if you say so.' Roland fished a ball out of his pocket and made it dance. 'I've got the only two balls worth having. The rest have been in and out of Trixie's mouth once too often. Bags me and Rose against you two. I have to warn you, Mo, that young George's backhand's as weak as the proverbial H_2O.' He spun the racquet. 'Mo to serve to me. All set?'

They had been organised in short order because Roland was decisive, not because he was proving a point. Tennis was why they were here; the squirrel was separate. Rose knew it but had no time to understand. Now in the artificiality of games she was allied with him – George and Mo allied. Was life itself, the tedium of politics, the actualities of the RDC, of the Church of England all worked by temporary alliances? She didn't know. She knew nothing except how watchful she was since the bright little animal, the wiping out – brothers, fathers – and blood fading in the reviving tree.

Mixed doubles: awaiting Mo's serve, she tried to recall the rules about tramlines. Mo's stillness was coming into its own. Mo placed her feet, bounced the ball, hit it. It was nearly an ace and Roland muffed it. Her turn next. She had dressed for as much freedom as prettiness of effect allowed but limbs coming out of hibernation were a little stiff whereas tennis did not want the stiffening of sinews – wanted quick flowing about, pauses to judge action and get on the ball. This time Mo served up, if not a sitting duck, a duck with its mind on other things. Rose managed a very neat return to George who slashed out with a large helping of luck. Roland leapt to make a smash and was nearly on when Mo's racquet sent the speeding projectile into the furthest corner of Rose's half. 'It is "in", isn't it? In the tramlines I mean.' It was of course. Thirty/Love.

There was some talk of sets, references to Queen's Club, Wimbledon between the emergent experts, Roland and Mo. It was decided to play three games, then go at the refreshments. Then, if the match had not already been decided to settle it in two further games. 'Or one, because three to one would be unbeatable,' said George after the winning (by Mo) of the first game. Next was Roland's service and he demolished George with a variety of deliveries all perfectly within the rules, in textbook style. His 'sorries' and 'bad lucks' seemed unmarked by brotherly irony. Roland, Rose thought, was simply good at sorting out weakness and strength and responding, unmindful of George's mounting chagrin, appropriately. He was simply playing the game. Rose knew herself too poor a player to be troubled with giving quarter as Mo may have done for her. Third game and George to serve. Love/Forty and Rose gave George the *coup de grace* by a fluke return. Two games to Roland and one to Mo.

There was enough heat in the day and had been in the sport to make the idea of lemonade glugging over its single pebble rival all the waterfalls of Switzerland.

'Plays well,' announced Roland when they were all seated, backs against the springy mesh and pop bottles working.

'He can't mean me,' said Rose. 'I'm an all-round duffer.'

'No, you're not,' said Mo in support.

'My elder brother probably has in mind my prowess on the field of battle.'

'The court plays well, that's all. When compared to grass. And I speak as one whose college had a positive fanatic – "Boer War Bill" – one of those who offer a silver joey every time you find a leaf which isn't grass. Father was right to stick to asphalt.'

'If the summer turns out hot,' said Rose, 'everyone might stick to it.'

'No need to be sarky. It's been improved. I say, did I ever tell you I met father once out there? Had to salute him! Subaltern and Brigadier, quite a hoot. We *were* stuck – up to the ankles at least. Mud. No wonder the idea of a hard court appealed to Dad. Bit rum that father and son fought in the same war.'

'Still fighting it,' said George. 'Or each other.'

'Shouldn't say so.' Roland pulled a blade of grass through the wire and was cupping it between half open hands. 'Used to do this as a boy.' He blew a parping sound as sudden and unmusical as an old-fashioned motor horn.

'It is something to have in common, *that*.'

'The Great Bore War,' George explained to Mo, 'started approximately on my tenth birthday and is still going strong.'

Mo said: 'Let's talk about something else then. A boy – rather a nice boy … ' (the comment, thought Rose, from almost anyone else would have been artful) 'explained all this – psychoanalytical? – stuff to me once. Apparently everyone has a "subconscious" whether they know it or not!'

'By definition,' said George sagely.

'I don't know about that, but he explained subconscious associationism which means if someone says a word and then someone else says one, there's a connexion. Anyone can do it but you have to study for *years* to know what it means, the subconscious part of it.'

Rose backed her up. 'It sounds rather fun.'

'You serve me a word!' Now that it was word rather than action, George seemed relaxed for the first time that morning, alive and touched by the glow of April woodland. Roland seemed very much older, as if the War and his extra years had caught up with him or else that he was caught out with people too young for him. Mo and George were a possibility in Rose's mind; herself and Roland? Mere light thoughts from the Noah's Ark tendency she had in social situations. What was the word game Mo was suggesting?

'She's thinking too consciously, not *sub* enough!' George was being positively playful.

'Not!' Mo had been pulling her face into a frightful mask of cerebration. 'Anyway the first word doesn't have to be subconscious, that's the whole point. Me to serve up the first word and you to return the first one to come into your head. Got it? George first since he volunteered – then Roland picks up George's and Rose goes last. Ready? *Insects.*'

'Legs,' said George.

'Wire,' said Roland.

'Electric light.'

'Now we do it the other way round. You say a word, Rose, then it goes to Roland, then George and finally me.'

Rose closed her eyes. 'A girl trying to think is a study in itself,' she heard George saying.

'Get on with it.'

'*Blood.*'

'Black,' said Roland.

'Night,' said George.

'Death,' said Mo.

'My father always says psychowotsit's morbid,' said Rose. 'So don't go proposing it to your Uncle John, dear girl!'

'Come on. Get it over with!' Roland took Rose's hand to assist her up. His was cool, dry, steady, solid. 'Your turn to throw them down this time.'

Her first was a fault but her second got it in the right area where it gave a triumphant hop, was gathered by Mo's neat backhand only to be smashed by Roland within an inch of the baseline. Fifteen/Love. Each of the next two points hovered on longish rallies and each was won by Roland and Rose – or more truly lost by George on a return which Roland now was absolutely placing for his brother not to muff. Rose crossed over to the right side wiping perspiration from her forehead.

'Match point I think,' said Roland.

'There's the fifth game.'

'Don't need it if we bag this one, young shaver.'

Rose who had been half-thinking the doddle shots Roland had produced were a brotherly gift to Hallet minor had no time to examine her half-thoughts. She was serving to Mo on the match point with no more interest in the outcome than skill to do other than try to clear the net and land on the right side of the centre line. To give the match away by deliberately double-faulting, thus ensuring a further game, yes it did enter her mind. But it was easier simply to do her best. That was to be a thing to think about repeatedly in future years, as too was Mo's reception of the slow and easy ball – Mo hardly moved at it. It was in the bag.

Roland expressed a futile wish for more pop. 'There's apples still.' Mo retrieved them from the foot of the mesh.

'Hang on.' George's foot had budged the army pack. He said, 'Pop!'

The revolver Rose saw clearly in his hand, the sudden hole in Mo. Ever afterwards she could unthread much of the horror but never heard the shot.

TOMORROW IS ANOTHER DAY

MAY 1961

'I'm going totally to reform – he said, then ... ' Godfrey laughed – it was painful and huge. 'Then he *died!* I ask you!' Godfrey had never been known to ask anybody anything in the way of an opinion. 'His refusal to split an infinitive was what got me. Jesus.' Godfrey looked at the bright window. 'Christ!'

The three recently appointed ones, his audience, sat in their best clothes. There was Tim in the wedding suit chosen a year before by his mother whilst he was returning from Africa; Marjorie was in something she was growing doubtful of, lapels and gussets slashed with black leather – the shop had goaded her into it though Janet (now premenstrually absent) had approved at the time, saying the design derived from Jacqueline Kennedy's style ... but as no other soul had commented in any way, the quavering voices she lived with were beginning to fill the gap; Bob Cupstock used his father's tailor and was grandly easy in herringbone. Their ages averaged out around twenty-five.

Godfrey's teaching service at the college was nearer forty in years, even allowing for the golden gap of the wartime commission in the RASC, stories of which, even to him, had become smooth through the action of years and repetition like stones on a beach. The *obiter dicta* he was now reporting were of much newer date though incredibly enough Larry Churchman had uttered them all of three years ago and thus passed away never knowing that Harold Macmillan, his indelible *bête noir*, had swept the polls. At least Larry had been saved that. It had been the old building then and a different common room. Larry had once visited the site of this smart monstrosity though and standing in what was to become the Grand Foyer had proposed an astounding list of objects – and people – he'd like to see buried in propitiation. This new room contained a few pieces from its predecessor, for example the massive sideboard gifted by the Founder and familiarly referred to as 'The Dame Eileen'. Godfrey clearly recalled back in the autumn of Suez Larry leaning on the Dame and excoriating the Government before a crowd of jingoes from Industry and Commerce whom the college was at that time out to impress with the virtues of 'day-release'. A fragment floated into Godfrey's mind which made reference to the present PM. 'If that man's grandpa was a crofter, then I'm a sheep's anus.' May's blind blue sky confronted Godfrey's realisation that he'd loved the man.

'He came before Mr Archer?' asked Tim helpfully. 'I mean as Head of the General Studies Department?'

'Larry created it,' said Godfrey. 'Before Larry it was like bits of protoplasm in the primeval soup, to take my metaphor from the Catering Department. There was Commercial French here, a scrap of Double-entry there and the things that went on in the Annexe – sex education, that sort of stuff. Now we do London External and there's A-level work. Larry created it and Archer's destroying it.'

They looked hesitant disbelief. Of course, Archer had appointed them – they were his creatures! But Godfrey immediately baulked at his thought: they were younger, less than half his own age, that was all. To them it was all ancient history which to him explained everything. Over the years Godfrey had protected himself from the worst the world could do – that at least. Robustly, that had been what Larry had stood for and understood, kicking things aside in pure, towering humane rage. Larry had always raised things to the power of 'n', whatever that was. Godfrey now wished kindly to let the three off the hook of his rambling attempt to pass on wisdom; abashed by insight, he fumbled round to do it, finally alighting on the young woman's unusual attire.

'That's a cracking outfit, Mabel. Not seen anything like it since we had a Czechoslovakian bomb-disposal unit billeted on us.'

There was a questing moment of silence before Marjorie exploded into tears and out of the room. The door – fitted as all were with the over-efficient 'British Strongarm' device – snapped shut behind her.

'The poor girl,' said Bob urbanely as only he could, 'is having real trouble with C2Z and with the Butchers.'

'Bomb-disposal's about right then.' Godfrey was baffled.

'If you'd allow a word from a very junior colleague,' said Bob, 'well, women are very sensitive in matters of dress. Unlike the gross male.' Bob crossed immaculately clad legs. Since Christmas his pleasant face had been furnished with a neat little moustache which from time to time he would blow into ruffling motion, as he did now.

'It's a pity Janet's not here to pull Marjorie out of the Ladies,' Tim commented.

Part of the tidying ordained these past weeks by the Vice-Principal had cleared all notice boards apart from the ubiquitous 'Briefing Document' with today's date, so long coming and now arrived, boldly stencilled. Miss Chives, mouselike lieutenant and companion to Miss Hutchings, had taken refuge in furious housework-like activity. Those tempted to cosmic speculation detected an unfairness in the timing of Miss Hutchings's illness, an affliction with fatal overtones from what gossip gleaned to feed on. Miss Hutchings was one of very few to remember Dame Eileen in the flesh and, herself a woman of forceful presence, high intelligence and the ability to groom Purpose with humour, could bring the Founder to life on the formal occasion. In direct line of descent as it were, Emily Hutchings had completed Dame Eileen's work and what had started out against the odds by effort of the great suffragist in bits of rooms and churchy halls had grown now in the century's seventh decade into a building full of gleaming equipment, potplants, 'British Strongarms', noisy youngsters who knew no better than to take for granted the Further Education yielding up the sweet fruition of a piece of paper – City & Guilds, HNC, even – as Godfrey had remarked – a London External BA. It was an irony therefore that Emily Hutchings was not to be the one receiving the Royal Personage but in her stead her constant companion and colleague, poor fussy Miss Chives. Nervous when not in her hideaway (reversible notice on the door 'WORKING' or 'AVAILABLE'), Miss Chives had coped with glory in her own way. The student body with the exception of its Union Exec had been left to snore away the royal morning in its beds; car parks were free of cars and had been thrice swept. As long ago as March when May had seemed a blue illusion there had been a plea from Miss Chives – who must by then have known the true cause of the Principal's absence – to leave one's car at home. Bob, Janet, Tim, Marjorie and the anarchic Bill Watts who together made up the new staff intake had occupied the back rows of Lecture Theatre A8 and disbelievingly registered the nervous admonition to come in on The Day 'by public convenience'. For weeks they had deeply enjoyed the phrase – impressing Godfrey, and others, how young these were, how old those were becoming.

'There's something,' said Bob, 'not quite right about this.'

'What's that?' Godfrey dug himself up from futile, unspecific revery.

'I think I must have misread instructions or been misinformed,' said Bob. 'There's an air of misplacement, don't you think? Here we are – but where is everybody else?'

'Marjorie's in the Ladies,' suggested Tim. 'We could knock, unless she's been collared for duties ... I could see ... '

There had been various changes of plan. Miss Chives had followed the instincts of Domestic Science which most of all meant subjecting things to a good seeing-to; the banishing of untidiness had like many another outbreak started in the kitchens to spread stage by stage through all craft rooms; with such official encouragement, the obsessiveness of trades became outvying and spangled the life of the college; as for General Studies something when Miss Chives got to it (the essential scruffiness of the human mind maybe) beached her energies. The General Studies Department had been ordered to stand by for general duties. Once a comforting notion, now with zero hour minutes away, having nothing to do, no sound of activity elsewhere – it was all becoming ominous, unsettling. Tim and Bob simultaneously consulted watches, Tim's a wedding present from his Nigerian father-in-law putting twenty-two jewels on his wrist; Bob's an heirloom hauled from the pocket. They exchanged pale smiles.

Godfrey had nodded off. But Marjorie's appearance startled them all up flights of consciousness. She had on a dress floriferously mauve and green and on her head someone's Millinery finals. Her face in the middle was marked by weeping. Bob Cupstock rose to his feet. 'What a brilliant ensemble! Hot work getting it by the deadline. You wash and brush up and I shall scout.' Bob's stronger British arm held sway and Marjorie left again, this time almost certainly to powder her nose.

'Charm the balls off a gnat,' remarked Godfrey appreciatively, sinking back into the chair he favoured, one known if not in his hearing as the 'God-slot'. The tag was the invention of Bill Watts who claimed connection with the world of television and came up with phrases weeks or months later to be heard in public discourse. 'God-slot' apparently was how religious broadcasting was known to up-and-coming young atheistical producers.

Tim now virtually on his own crossed to the window. The college buildings at least had the beauty of newness, at most – despite standard-issue scepticism – an oddity, even charm in comparison to blocks ugly as money beginning to rise over harmless, accustomed skylines. Already there was a myth that the architect, stuck for inspiration, had fiddled out his design at the breakfast table from a toast rack and an egg, presumably poached in one of those tin-hat arrangements. The egg was the dome of the dining areas, presently visible at a steep angle. Beyond, the scene was surprisingly verdant, not in the fashion of the West African bush but in full new leaf and set off by drifts of may-blossom whiter than any lace, even when worn by Elspeth. Tim's eyes were truanting into nature as rendered by generations of English poets. Elspeth at home with her unchanged nervousness of this (new to her) old country and its white-faced city rush; here (only not today) the students, grabby, careless but vital as well: all the people in Tim's life relaxed their pressure for a green moment in Tim's head.

Godfrey groaned and stirred in his slot but did not wake, for Bob Cupstock was one of few whose entries and exits went unmarked by clump or bang. 'Timothy,' he said joining him at the window, 'you'll never guess, old thing, what's gone and happened.'

'The four-minute warning?'

'Nothing so simple I'm afraid, no.'

'Kennedy's been killed?'

'More domestic,' said Bob. 'You know I followed Marjorie out? Well, I left her in the capable hands of Sylvia Weston – you know, on the Student Exec. Quick face-job in the salon, Sylvia's a bit of an artist. Then I found Archer whimpering in a corner.'

'Archer whimpering?'

'Suicidal clucking's perhaps a better way of putting it. He had just discovered something. Namely, Timothy, that Miss Chives got one detail rather badly wrong. It's tomorrow – the royal schedule has us down for *tomorrow*.'

'But the students will be back!'

'Yes, that should make the place more lively.'

'What a cock-up, Bob!'

'I had a bit of a chat with Mr Archer and we're deeming this a dress rehearsal – sufficient unto the day sort of thing. The General Studies Department is to provide the platform party and no one will notice the difference. Talk about lese-majesty.'

'What about Godfrey?'

'Leave the poor old soul.'

Miss Chives, the worst having been feared for her, had been brought round almost into believing that a dress rehearsal had been intended all along. This feat had been achieved of all people by Bill Watts, severely reformed it seemed by the dynamic Mrs Copley of Hairdressing. There had been talk of an illicit affair but more positively here was proof of Woman's redemptive power as manifest in the newly groomed appearance. Tim mused along these lines as he waited with the others outside revolving doors now folded back, and strained his vision the length of the red carpet to the little tableau of the reception committee. Bob and Bob's gold heirloom were in charge. Inexplicable, thought Tim reliving the horrors of getting the FO wallahs in Lagos to process Elspeth's papers, that Bob was here and not in the Diplomatic Service.

'We would actually be arriving in two minutes' time,' said Bob, 'police escorts having brought the whole town to a standstill. Marjorie, Your Royal Highness, I'm your equerry and Sylvia is Lady Sylvia in waiting. Tim here's the detective.'

'One doesn't need to be instructed.' Marjorie sounded as if she meant it.

'We simply walk down to the reception committee and then through into the Hall where the consort of viols does its stuff. The plaque's the usual sort of arrangement with tasselled string.'

'We are rather used to it,' said Marjorie.

'Off we go.'

Students of the Exec and cleaning ladies stood corralled behind red ropes. Tim was acutely conscious of them but the hand-clapping was just right in volume and tempo. His wallet heavy with things other than money jostled his armpit to remind him that it was a shoulder holster; his fingers he found to be significantly cusped on loose-hanging arms. They had covered the distance with nothing more menacing than the quick unfurling of the Exec's CND banner.

'Alderman Scrimgeour, my Lord Mayor: Ma'am.'

'This is a right how-do,' said the Alderman.

'How do you do?' Marjorie gave his chain of office a fingertip regal blessing. 'I do hope this is easy to keep clean.'

'Man hours likely. Solid silver inset with gold.'

'It suits you, if one may say so.'

'Thanks very much, Ma'am.'

The Lady Lord Mayoress curtseyed and Marjorie deftly passed to Sylvia a simple spray of seasonal flowers. Bob next introduced the Director of Education, Mr Keate, who was said in the higher gossipy circles to possess just enough intelligence to exploit his natural stupidity. He was a shifty little fellow, not eased by Marjorie's next gracious remark: 'I have seen your name on vans.'

She asked all five Heads of Department pertinent questions, calling Mr Archer 'Mr Churchman' twice, without batting a Sylvia-coated eyelid. Mrs Copley of Hairdressing – whether as self-deluding as most of her trade's clients, or just voluble, or somehow in support of the trimmed Bill Watts who had slunk off, or just a good sport – had set the tone by giving an excellently succinct account of her job. Mr Duddon of Catering emulated her; Miss Baxter-Forbes of Dressmaking (who was known to have 'difficulties' with Miss Chives) had kept her Department in the picture; Mike Merle of Hotel Management was merely professionally superb; which left Mr Archer or 'Churchman' as Marjorie had oddly chosen to call him. Which finally left Miss Chives.

Here Marjorie transcended the mounting expectations of her entourage. She took both of Miss Chives's frail hands in hers. 'Really, how *is* Miss Hutchings? Such a richly *earned* OBE.'

'I'm afraid for her.' The millinery obscured the next exchange from their attendant ears. It was of some length, spoken quietly and registered in the Vice-Principal's ordinary worthy face, never before known as a landscape for emotional lights and shades. Bob's timing held and he coughed equerrily. So HRH and Miss Chives led the procession on into the Great Hall. The consort of viols augmented by a small detachment of the Royal Air Force Band gave a rendition of the earliest known setting of the National Anthem. Again there was applause, a spring shower of it. More red carpet led up to the focus of the proceedings, a daïs and a microphone. Marjorie mounted the one and took the other. The music passed away, tenderly setting free a silence of expectancy. With an equally perfect timing, Marjorie spoke.

'This is a fine season to open a fine building. I know how many people have worked and for how long. It is a great sadness to us that Miss Emily Hutchings OBE is unable to be with us today, a great sadness.' Marjorie fell silent. Poor sick Miss Hutchings grew in the thoughts of all, but Bob – Tim could tell – for the very first time was becoming jumpy. She was out of cough-shot, out of elbow-touch, on her own, exposed, beyond their keeping.

'The college is open,' she said – no longer in the voice of an HRH

___ MONTHS ___

at all, but in her own more nasal, more familiar, never-listened-to voice. 'It is open from nine to nine every day except Saturdays and holidays ... *for forty years* ... ' Her knees gave, but slowly. Even Bob did nothing.

Mrs Copley streaked to catch the falling colleague, ably assisted by Deirdre Baxter-Forbes who came a close second. The RAF was becoming flummoxed.

Bob said: 'The Red Lion's open. Let's get there. Quick.'

REVELATIONS

JUNE 1951

U-shaped, V-shaped? William's eyes were very tired. He was exhausted, glaciation on the brain, in the head. It had been a successful field day, *might* have been ... An hotel for once: a real relief after all the hostelling. The Stalborg skilfully perched in 1937 at the top of the valley must have been an amazing home from home for officers of the invading *Wehrmacht*. For William just now sitting on its broad wooden terrace it was simply comfort to let tired sight clamber amongst the rounded domes suddenly eroding at aeon speed in the thickening swill of Scandinavian summer night. Of course, near as could be a classic 'U'.

Lynne's bright voice afar, settling the kids.

Two thirds of the way through the fortnight and one out of twenty missing. five per cent was good wartime odds but damned bad school-teaching odds: what the press would label 'Unacceptable'. The squadron had seen Norwegian service but that had been long before his stint. William had been meaning to check whens and wheres but had simply not found the time. These five minutes to himself were quite warm enough to sit outside while the globe inched down the wick of the sun for brief June shut-eye. His pipe, an old infrequent habit, was fished out. This if anywhen called for the smoke of meditation.

And it might aid concentration on Winship.

Still wrapped in a baize apron, the old codger had fetched out an oil lamp which he fiddled with to blossom into a simulchrum of the absent moon. 'Ha det så bra.'

'Carry on.' William waved his pipe. The old man, presumably from his apron, flourished out three small glasses and like an elderly Danny Kaye placed them – one, two, three.

'Takk.' The man withdrew with a smile and a bow. He was what they used to call 'a humorist'; perhaps it was some parody of his own not so long no doubt after waiting on members of the Master Race. Norwegian humour was the most profound of their national secrets.

When going, the pipe drew like a dream in the still, moist air, its issue encircling the lamp: moon riding clouds on the table instead of up in the undifferentiated sky. A military step known from RAF days was that of Captain Staaland, seen earlier on. William cranked his troublesome back.

'I only am reporting no progress and I am calling more other automobiles in the search.'

'Please be seated.'

Staaland placed his police cap next to the lamp. A heavy man of about forty, he was weary either from the day or from the long strain of living perhaps on the run from the invaders and seeing God knew what

– more than had come William's younger way in the control towers of Yorks and Lincs. The Captain's uniform was blue and silver, adding to one's confidence in the man and further supporting an impression that Norway was a country which knew what it was doing. 'So we are having eight polices looking for your young man.'

'Algie Winship's only thirteen you know. It's a rum age.'

'"Rum age" is good.' Captain Staaland wrote it in his book.

'Boys of that age – I don't know, inside they're a mass of doubts. It's the group really, acceptance and all that.'

The officer got to his feet. It was Lynne approaching together with the old boy through the thinly settled night; the old boy placed a bottle next to the hat. She must have showered and was wearing a dress perhaps classifiable as 'New Look'. William who had never considered female attire his field saw perfectly familiar Lynne transformed into someone wholly unknown, a process oddly assisted by the captain's solid but easy courtesy. Northern, he shook rather than kissed her hand.

William explained: 'Mrs Bayard is my teaching colleague on the tour. It's a boys' school but still has one or two women staff left over from the war – emergency trained, I mean.'

'Some good out of that time is good.'

'Well, yes I suppose so.' He was trying to follow the thought.

'Thanks very much!' Lynne produced a school drama sniff.

'My men will call all farmers and persons living here. That time was training for finding people and hiding people. So, *vi ville si adjø*. But first the kind thought of Henrik. I am sorry that it is Swedish. Akvavit. Otherwise it is very good.' He filled the three glasses. 'Skål to the uncovery of Master Vinship!'

'Cheers.'

'*Tusen takk* – for everything,' said Lynne.

The Captain departed, Lynne sat on the chair William had pulled out for her. The spirit's fiery nip glowed in him like a filament but as he sat the absent Winship sat down with him. 'Little beggar must know what trouble he's causing, *have known* if he's done for himself.'

'What on earth do you mean?'

'Search me ... Knocked himself cold, been eaten by trolls.'

'You are worried then?'

'Course I am! Losing kids gets to the Education Committee, not to mention into the bloody *Daily Mirror*.'

'About *him*,' said Lynne, 'about Algie.'

'Oh, I see what you mean. Poor little beggar, what do we really know?'

'You can imagine what they're like up there. Quietly abuzz.'

'Hoping for something gruesome.'

'Partly.' She refilled their glasses. 'Partly it's more complicated. They showed me his things.'

'And?'

'There's always – I don't know – something a bit pathetic about a person's things.'

William set down his extinct pipe. 'God, think of sending them back to the Winship parents! One of my jobs at Leeming was to return effects of blokes who'd gone for a Burton.'

'There was this.' She placed before them a small red diary. In gold on the cover was the word EAGLE together with a picture of one a little like the RAF's but flying off sideways like Winship. 'It's from that new comic paper,' she said.

William turned up today's date, Wednesday, June 27th 1951. He said, 'Wednesday's child is full of woe. I don't know what they mean by that.'

'Mean by what?' As Lynne peered forward the swing of her hair brushed slightest tiptoe on his cheek.

'That Valentine bowls like Washbrook.'

There was the young Jamaican cricketer's photograph printed in the right-hand bottom corner. 'You're as bad as the boys! It's what poor Algie may have written we're looking for.'

'Nothing today of course, yesterday … their writing's like the dancers at the Windmill – a lot to be desired.'

Lynne seemed to snort. 'William! Today's a bit of a revelation. Give it here, *I* can read it. "Finished library book. Muddled." Does it mean the book or Algie?'

'Search me.'

'Don't keep saying that.'

'All right, Miss, you're i/c this investigation.' He liked watching her active hands.

'He did manage three days of new-year resolution at the beginning. "Cat getting better. Snow on ground. fiddled about. Went to town." Then nothing till the seventeenth of this month. "Didn't sleep much. Lights, heat and noise on ship. Dock in Ebsborough."'

'*Esbjerg*. The little blighters can't get anything right. I sometimes think teachers are masochists. Why didn't I stay at home and rest on the laurels of the French trip?'

'You wouldn't be here with me for one thing.'

'I don't know what to make of that. Do you?'

'Search me. This *is* odd. See.' Her slender finger, sensibly manicured, pointed to a *C* recurring three or four times for the past week with its detailings of 'Mountaineous scenery quite good'; 'Caught train for Voss.'

'It's a sign of some sort.'

'Well, I can't say "search me", can I?' William trapped her hand in his. It remained quiescent. In thirty years of life he had never sufficiently considered the eyes of another, what they signalled, the dark enterprise of another's being. It spun him.

'The last one,' she said, relentless, female, 'was against that train journey yesterday.'

'I see what you mean.' They stared at the documentary evidence, not cooked up in retrospect ... a footprint in the snow because that was where the foot went. It was night and not night, it was a dusk which at some point would become a dawn. The lamp on the table burned between. Signs of the missing boy's life.

'Winnie, Winnie, Winnie.' Cresswell would never ever stop. Algie looked across him out at the mountains. Men had carved this track out of the side of rock and there were sudden black tunnels. He'd tried to get another seat. They were in fours and opposite were Stark and Martin.

'Winnie won the war,' said Stark.

'Did you, Winnie?' asked Cresswell. 'Or was it your sister Winnie, Winnie?'

'That ninny in a pinny?' Jimmy Martin laughed at his own brilliance, they all laughed. Algie too – he didn't mind laughs when you could join in. His pursuer was Cresswell but the others weren't so bad: Stark could be what Grandpa called 'kosher' about art and Jimmy was wizard at Aircraft Recognition. It had all started at Harwich and had not stopped.

'I'm the only one.' Algie's parents had been quite old to marry and had explained once how ladies reach an age when they couldn't make babies any more. That was when he'd really thought about the fact of brothers and sisters, a few years ago. Funny how you took everything for granted and then some obvious or accepted thing turned different. Cresswell he had avoided by instinct since going into separate forms in second year. And then you learned what's what. Not just Cresswell; he had the idea of England over the horizons moored somewhere in space, in the sky even, far off with home in it, his mother in it – impossibly far away. An ache like tummy or tooth but worse and out of reach of first or second or third aid. It came and went though.

Cresswell sang: '"O, O Antonio, he's gone away/I'm all alonio, all on my ownio ... " My name's not Tony, Winnie, and I'm not going away.'

'You're the only what?' asked Martin genuinely.

'I mean I don't have a sister.'

'Oh, I see.' Martin turned to Stark and said in an ordinary way. 'Winship doesn't have a sister.'

'Neither do I,' said Stark, adding, 'It's not the end of the world.'

Algie felt immensely grateful. Roger Stark, the least known, liked art and was a Christian or had been talking such things over with Marshall who was definitely a Christian and not just a church-going one. Marshall said your life had to become a sort of church and they'd all laughed at the idea saying things like you'd need a notice over your ear: 'All offerings gratefully received towards the upkeep of the life herein.' Marshall had laughed as well. That was when he'd treated everybody to cakes and stuff after finding five pounds in Danish kroners at the hostel in Odense. Marshall was a good person; but having to go to the lavatory at Oslo station had resulted in not getting a seat near him but ending up in the worst place possible, next to Cresswell, who now said: 'What if Winnie had a sister? What would she be like, Martin?'

'Depends how old.'

'Use your imagination. Can't mean younger, can I? What age do you like them?'

'I see,' said Martin. 'My cousin's sixteen.'

'And has she?' Cresswell.

'Has she what?' Martin was puzzled but it was Cresswell making the running as he always did.

'Got her breasts up?'

Stark said, 'I say, why not leave Jimmy's cousin alone?'

'I'm not touching her.' The train rushed through a small tunnel. 'I'm touching up Winnie.'

'Through her pinny.' Martin hadn't forgotten his success.

'With my red hot cock,' said Cresswell. 'Speaking of which, Winnie, what's your considered opinion of Ma Bayard?'

'What do you mean?'

'Do up your flies.' Cresswell's quick hand reached out and with a deft tweak landed where the talk had caused a stirring in Algie's short trousers. Heat rushed into his face; Stark had noticed it, he could see that in Stark's face but also that he was not going to blab, the little battle of decision in Stark's face. Hot, sudden unbelieved-in prickly tears ascended but he stopped their fall and felt them sink back. Cresswell went in for one of his famous imitations, this time from the old ITMA programme. '"It's being so cheerful what keeps me going!" I'm not talking about scragging,' he said. 'I'm talking about the Real Thing. Careless talk costs lives so I need to know exactly where they are this moment now. Have a gander, Jimmy.' Martin obediently stood to look up and down the train which had the usual funny Scandinavian arrangement where they'd forgotten to put the compartments in. 'Just William's with Marshall. Mrs B is at the far end with Jenkins and that lot.'

'Right,' said Cresswell, 'listen in. You too, Winnie, specially you.' They bent their heads forward like a rugby scrum, Cresswell as usual in possession of the ball. Eyes craning upwards wove a mesh of expectant sight. 'Remember that hostel a couple of nights back – think it was Sweden – where the showers were across a sort of courtyard?'

'Grottlingholm,' said Stark.

'Something like that. You must've thought I'd gone on the trip into Stockholm, didn't you, Winnie?'

'The Old Town?' It was true and it was why Algie had elected to stay behind with the washers-up.

'That's where you're mistaken then,' said Cresswell. 'I went sightseeing.'

'Come off it,' said Stark. 'Just now you said you didn't.'

'There's sights and sights.' Cresswell was pleased with himself, having trapped their curiosity on the end of his line. 'The sight I saw is not a hundred kilometres from here, except it's now got its clothes on.'

'Wait a minute ... '

Cresswell was vivid with delight – he squeezed Jimmy's knobbly knee. 'The krone's dropping, is it?'

'Not Ma Bayard?'

'Those showers were wood and wood's got knotholes, has it not? You remember the old dire rhyme which goes "In days of old when knights were bold/And women not invented/Men bored holes in telegraph poles ... "'

'Get on with it.' Stark's tongue was half poking out.

'Waiting turns that afternoon, I did a tour of inspection. The women's showers had one plank right height with a whopping knothole which, if you're like me and carry a knife, didn't take men working shifts to ... prise out ... replace till needed. I heard *Lynne* asking about the hot water situation. It was all right from six. "*Sex*" was how the old party told her. Little me was there quarter to.'

'Did you see anything?'

'Not *anything*, Jimmy – *everything*.'

'Knickers?'

'Even Winnie here doesn't keep his knickers on. She's not that ancient really and she is an eyeful. I saw her public hair.'

'What's that?'

'Round you-know-what, private parts. Suppose that's why it's called "public" for some daft reason. You listening, Winnie?'

Algie did a sort of bobbing nod. Mrs Bayard had always been kind to him and – it must have been just after that shower at Grottlingholm – had gone out of her way for a chat, asking if he was all right. He had vowed never to let her down; in some way withstanding the torment of Cresswell was easier than receiving Mrs Bayard's concern. Now Cresswell had been everywhere with the muck of his hands and eyes.

'So you see,' said Cresswell, 'there's sightseeing and there's seeing sights. The things on her tits, there's red round them the size of half-crowns. Bet not many people know that.'

'Bet Just William does!'

Convulsions at the thought – Martin's hand over his mouth with sounds squirming out like worms between his fingers. Algie sensed his own head hanging in the manner of the barrage balloons of early memory. Cresswell's turned sideways to fork a triumphant look. 'Winnie does not approve of our lascivious levity.' He had such phrases from his music-hall imitations. 'Not sweet on her, are we?'

'You're not,' said Algie. 'That was dirty.'

'No *that* wasn't. *That* was pink and soapy and ... ' Cresswell made a heavy grunting noise. 'Change places with Algie, Stark, would you?' They moved round and now Algie was opposite Cresswell who said, 'Your turn for a window-seat.'

'My knee gets locked,' said Stark, rubbing it. Mountains passed.

'You change with me, Jimmy,' said Cresswell.

Algie looked out of his window: now he was between the devil and the deep blue sea. They were all in the same positions, only reversed. It was like musical chairs. With Cresswell you never knew what until it happened to you.

You could escape a bit by staring through the big window until you felt the mountains striding your eyesight, your eyes free of the train and out of Cresswell's reach. And Algie's mind was finding open country, new knowledge growing over what he knew – that Cresswell was somehow blind and – as mountains lapped and rippled into higher, dimmer levels ... and that sometime, somehow someone would pity Cresswell for it. These were the lightest of ideas floating off in cloud. Nearer, more width was opening out from the track with small fields, houses many with roofs covered in turf. He smiled at the notion of his mother telling Dad to mow the roof. A goat grazing by a chimney was so extraordinary that he nearly mentioned it – until he remembered.

Roger was getting out his playing cards.

'Just a tick,' said Cresswell. He'd suddenly edged up. 'Half a mo.' Algie thought of mowing the roof. He was being pressed in by

Cresswell's steady sideways force and because his arms had been quietly angled to his sides he was pinioned now between Cresswell and the side of the carriage. 'Winnie wants his shoes off. He wants us to smell his feet. Undo his laces, would you? He said Lynne was dirty flesh.'

'I didn't!'

'Shut up, there's a good chap.'

Martin was untying his laces and though there was still freedom in his legs to kick out he did not; apology was in the fingers through which the power of Cresswell's blind force had squirmed. He was locked in though.

'Take a quick sniff, Jimmy, but don't overdo it. Unclean flesh test.'

As his shoe came off, Algie made one shuddering try. Martin started back but Cresswell didn't budge an inch. There was the thin figure of Marshall hovering over them. 'Anything up?' he mildly enquired.

'We were thinking of cards,' said Stark – Marshall was a junior prefect.

'I've heard of gamblers putting their shirts on but young Winship's putting his socks,' said Marshall pleasantly.

'It's an experiment,' said Cresswell. 'Winnie's helping out in an experiment. Or you could say we're playing Christians and Jews, bit like Cowboys and Indians, only you don't need the space. Space is just what you don't need actually.'

'I don't get your meaning.'

'I think you do,' said Cresswell, 'I think you do.'

'My advice is leave Winship alone.'

'All advice gratefully received. My advice is not to go bleating to J.W. or Ma Bayard. Unless that is, you want them to know about the Danish money you spent instead of handing it in. Stick to the Good Book's my advice, Marshall. There's plenty more where that came from.'

'I see,' said Marshall. He was tall for his age, pale and stuck hesitatingly by a thin hand on the back of Stark's seat. 'Are you all right, truly, Algernon?'

'I'm all right.'

'That's all right then,' said Marshall. He moved on back to his seat.

'When it comes down to it,' said Cresswell, 'your Holy Joes pass by on the other side. Put back his shoe, Jimmy. I'll sleep on it and maybe tomorrow we'll have real sport.'

'It must mean something.' Lynne's anxious, new-seen face. William landed a clumsy kiss, a greater surprise to him perhaps than to Lynne.

'I meant the sign, silly. Here. What did you think I meant, William?'

'Search me … It's just … It doesn't matter.'

'It does as well. Alex said to find myself somebody to go with to the Festival of Britain. He has to go to Aden and there's a spare ticket. There wouldn't be harm in it, if you wanted to. "Someone you get on with" was what he said. I think we do. But right now we need to decypher this diary.'

'I'll give it very best consideration. Thanks! You're a sport.' They bent studious heads, he looking back over his shoulder to unlit windows.

'That train journey yesterday, it must have been three hours. My intuition is telling me to talk with Christopher Marshall.'

'He's a reliable lad right enough, but I don't see how he could help ...'

'Unless ... Come on, I've got good ears.' She caught his hand and took him to the rail of the terrace.

On an inspiration, William – having to whisper it through her hair, said, 'You've got lovely ears.'

'Like seashells – I know. *Shh.*'

It was one of Captain Staaland's police automobiles snaking up the mountain road. Headlights flashed and horn hooted on rounding the final bend. It was Captain Staaland himself getting out of the unexpected driver's door. Emerging from the other, Algie Winship gave a sheepish wave.

Lynne gave William a quick, spontaneous embrace. 'Thank the Lord! I may be wrong, but I think that boy will be all right.'

TOO CLOSE FOR COMFORT

JULY 19 —

MONTHS

England is governed after dinner. It is then that matters of moment can usually be decided in an unminuted half an hour. Who was it said that our real national sport was Politics? Clever enough as a comment, I admit. To my mind though it is more the means – respectable and accepted – through which we indulge our secret interest in human nature. People and not ideas interest us: the power of the state is our universal Wembley Stadium.

You must know from the outset that I am not even a second-eleven man myself in these matters. Yet I have certainly been 'a supporter', one of the crowd for twenty years now at that annual July event, that Ascot/Henley of Politics which takes place at Maria's. Maria, you will know who I mean – the newspaper pictures of her, her voice on the radio; but in the pictures the animation of life is missing, and making 'This Week's Good Cause' appeal on the BBC she is a disembodied voice. I go (or always went) for Maria in the flesh. Twenty years of such a gathering is a record in my view and for nineteen of them I found myself happily seated on the sidelines. Is my telling you about the twentieth an attempt at exorcism?

As ever, the weather is good. When we were younger we had fun with the idea that Maria arranged it with the Almighty and once she upstaged us – many years ago now – by producing *Cantuar*, a jolly old cove. This year the young are worried which becomes annually more tiresome and unsettling. I politely agree on the direness of the universe and make my way out of doors. Bats which have always been welcome at Maria's are sewing up their suppers under a small yellow moon. Away from the house, I come across a member of Cabinet being sick and ask if he's all right. He says, 'Don't quote me.'

To light one of my cheap cigars, I locate a marble bench in the summery gloom. Being on one's own can be sweeter than a patriotic death. This July, apart from the military equipment affair, the scandal is about governmental bending of rules to let truly dubious foreigners buy slabs of London. Each summer it is something. Stirred by the Press and laced with legal and other plums, there is always a confiture many cannot resist. Some make off with the jam and others come unstuck (or forever stuck) with money lost or closed careers. Fame and fortune and sugar water!

Now fades the slight departing crunch over Maria's raked gravel. Now gently swells the not unpleasant pop band organised by her younger son. Her house and grounds here where I am may be familiar to you, probably through the medium of television. Maria's has featured in two 'ads', one mini-series as well as the major adaptation.

Purpose-built by an ancestor of the dunderhead husband, it has always witnessed Money meeting Class. Not being purchasable, you will know, is the stock-in-trade of Class – and also that it goes like hot cakes when wrapped in inverted commas. By which I intend no inverted snobbery; for twenty years Maria for me has been in a class of her own. She has to live! Picture me then on my marble slab, smoking my maudlin cigar in that state which both knows and doubts its validity. Desolate moments in which we all secretly meet are not properly to be spoken of.

I am forty-three now, of good family – Gerard William Mayn Arblet by name, but known as Gerry. Our recorded history ends – I should say *begins* – somewhat before the Conquest. According to my Aunt Helen Mayn, Aethelbert was a forebear who landed in Kent and subdued the local Inland Revenue, a knack I have not inherited. Always old-fashionedly truthful, she did add that Aethelbert was 'slightly removed'. Fame was mine at five years old when I said I felt him *entirely* removed. Never have I recaptured that pinnacle with Mother and her sister repeating to each other my celebrated riposte. With the exception of two occasions with Maria, that moment was undoubtably the most comfortable station of my cross. In total contrast to what was to follow! I have sketched my marble musings to give you my general situation when arrived the Lady whom I cannot by any means name.

'Don't tell me what you're called and for God's sake don't get up. What you can do is something to smoke.'

My cheap cigars happen to carry the Appointment; matchlight plays over that face. Dishevelled is what she is and agitated. Inhaling, she disburdens smoke and confidences. 'I had the best of the swine, don't care what's said. Damn think positive, wouldn't you say? Face the facts. People change. The late twenties, not everyone's best stretch by a long chalk. Think of —' (here she refers to a wearer of the Diadem but Royalty, more than most, treats the long-dead as if they are contemporaries) ... 'Well, the poor dear spent *his* late twenties literally in the shithouse. Turned thirty, he faced up and made no end of a go. With —' (the famous one on her dishevelled mind) 'I had the best of him. Opposite case altogether until he hit the Big Three. God, he was funnier than the Palladium, generous as the welfare state. In a four-poster he was a *rave* – or anywhere else he could get it. Thirty – funeral march all the way. Bloody newspapers lapped it up but they didn't have to sleep with him. Not like ... ' Flicking the butt of my humble cigar ten yards, she censors herself this time and changes the subject. 'Did I see the FO man cruising this neck of the woods?'

I say: 'To put it diplomatically, he did pass by a few minutes ago.'

'*Pass by!*' In the sillier papers she is known for many things but, closer to, her reputation is for laughs and *looks* which freeze ornamental water and bring down game birds in or out of season. Now to my great consternation, she grabs my knee. 'He spewed it diplomatically into yon herbaceous border.' I feel the grip of ringy fingers. 'You know the clear-out PMs go in for about now?'

'Reshuffles,' I gasp.

'They chuck dead wood and hopeless young hopefuls. It's common knowledge Spookytooth's for the chop.' I have an unhelpful vision of my blood supply being turned off, my leg falling on the gravel. She continues: 'I need to know if that thrusting Scottish laddie will get his job. There's some bounder here called Partridge or Drake who knows these things. Plus more MPs than spare proverbials and then the FO man. Constitutionally, I can't ask a thing. Do I make myself clear at all? You look sound I must say. Do I know you?'

'Gerry Arblet, Ma'am.' She releases my knee.

'Father played some polo?'

'Not very well, I'm afraid.'

'You'll do!' She gives a final slap. 'You'll do it! I stay a half an hour and I must get ten minutes with Maria. She cheers me up and bloody few things do.'

There is no mistaking such a command. The 'laddie' referred to was two years behind me at Worcester, MP and – significantly – former crony of the celebrated provider of four-poster fun. *Lackaday* is a useful old word fallen out of use.

My father who has always avoided polo did sit in the House for half a lacklustre Session and his tip on recognising MPs ('like prime Hampshire bacon') has always stuck in my mind. I see the 'laddie' silhouetted in one of the french windows which Maria – tastefully I have contended against that aside in Pevsner – had inserted along the garden side of the Great Hall. He looks pleased with himself – prime Ayrshire perhaps. On a hot July night Maria's windows ease the transfer from ceiling to stars, but she is famous for her unstuffy approach. She assumes no fellow creature better nor worse than herself. I can recall when she mixed in some locals one year and how surprised she was at the unease between them and other guests! Fond recollections! She lit little dying conversations; she rushed back with another match. Father met her once only and was critical only in one comment – 'That woman tries to make everything right for everybody.' I digress into sweeter pastures. My object is to glean information; my method must be to eavesdrop on political talk.

It is no task for a summer night. A politico on his – or more promisingly on *her* – own can be witty, even interesting. Two, you are in danger of hustings. The promotion of self and party line requires the big meeting, or the small screen.

What a relief to find that the hand on my arm belongs to Tom Summerbell, a backbencher to whom none of the above applies!

'Gerry! Tell me, where's the conservatory?'

We gain what I happen to know to be Maria's favoured spot. It was here once that she told me ...

I ask Tom how things are and am given a nip in a silver cup.

'My bloody seat,' says Tom, 'is Surrey with a fringe on top, said fringe being a very sticky bit of the Great Wen. About as much solid support there as water in the Gobi. Gerry, pity us poor bastards! All right, neither would I from the outside. "Posturing, rabbiting turds!" is what I'd say.'

'Relax, Tom. This time of year you all get jumpy.'

'Nothing gets to you, does it? It's what I like about you, Gerry.' It is meant as a compliment. 'My two marriages,' he goes on (he *is* a politician), 'both mistakes. Don't get me wrong, mistakes for the girls, sorry, *women*. Error singular: *me*. Did I say "singular"? Dozens of decent blokes in the House toiling, moiling, burning the midnight whatnot. All for why? The wind changes, someone farts. Widows, orphans, blind folk – whatever you've been sweating your bollocks off to sort out – gone, whipped into outer darkness. Don't ask me where: the ice-house at Balmoral, wherever you like. Sorry, sorry. Your Maria still pulls them in.'

'She's rather excelled even herself.'

'You carry the old torch?' Tom can surprise me.

'Be that as it may,' I say.

He guffaws professionally. 'Never thought to hear that phrase outside the Palace of Westminster! Half of it's here, mind. Saw the big Foreign man. My creepy parliamentary neighbour has hopes in that direction.'

'Does he?'

'Not a clue, have you, Gerry? The tartan monster sitting smugly on my northern border.'

'Just you follow me.' I lead him back into the Great Hall. The man in question is talking to the FO, a third party present, a moat of parquet surrounding them. This is not tittle-tattle.

Tom stretches to my ear. 'Hats-off time. Chief Whip. We are witnessing what some bright bugger once described as the most impressive sight on earth, a Scotsman getting on.'

'The Departmental job?'

'Shouldn't wonder. Now, let me see ... The sod got himself married last week.'

'Would I know the lady?'

'No. Shrewd bint in the Tea Room. Usual half-witted speculation at the time. Some said he'd done it to get served; others reckoned he wanted access to the ordinary English mind. She is a handsome woman ... How stupid! Someone was telling me he'd been deleted from the *Book of Record*.'

'Defence interests, wasn't it. Up in somewhere like Durham?'

'In one, old boy. Transferred his assets under the tea counter and up her pinny. Sanctimony is the first refuge of a rat.'

Short of time now, I say: 'Tom, don't ask me why, but I absolutely need to know if he's got this government job. *Absolutely*. Looks so, do you think?'

'Wouldn't tell me.' Tom Summerbell is one of those short-set, well-built, jovial Englishmen it's easy to underestimate. 'Lady in the case?'

'Entirely.'

'Pissing in the wind for you to ask him?'

'Graphically put. We've not been introduced. Oxford's too long back.'

'Case for Tucker Snipe.' Tom rubs the side of his nose. 'Give me a few mins on my own back in the greenhouse. I just need the presence of plants. You stay put.'

Staying put, I dimly think of Luther who also could do no other. But all is transformed when a serving-man brings me a tremendous glass of brandy. Maria has sent it across for me; I drink her and to her and for two minutes I forget the reality. Power's gravitation pulls all into its orbit. I can best understand by reaching back to the elemental, grabbing, criminal world of prep school (your elementary school playground would have been the same).

Who is Tucker Snipe? Into a diamond-flashing ear I must whisper, 'Yes, Ma'am' or 'It seems unlikely'. My fate is in the green fingers of Tom Summerbell. I am fighting a cowardly wish to flee back to the Royal Oak and hide in the leafy-wallpapered room annually so familiar to me.

I admit that the Arblets have always been on the sidelines of History and that I am a paradigm of indecisive centuries. Aunt Helen Mayn had not much to report following Aethelbert. We tilled land; we produced a few priests, but no bishops. There was Cuthbert in the eighteenth century but when his *Diaries* were published in 1903 they did not catch on. Cuthbert I am rather fond of. Once in Westminster Abbey for a great funeral he became ludicrously entangled with the pallbearers; once he fell down a well. She first in the public eye is now duly chatting to the lady first in mine. All time has nearly gone.

'Here.' It is Tom Summerbell, aglow with achievement. 'Take this envelope over to the Foreign Man. Inside, Tucker explains he's been asked by the PM to get a confirmation that the post has been accepted by the gravity-defying Jock. You're simply Tucker's messenger.'

'Who is Tucker Snipe?'

'Only the PM's most trusted *aide*. No one has seen him but they all know who he is.'

'Call me dim, Tom – I'm not with you.'

'It's why I always make sure to have my own stuff typed. Leaves my handwriting clear for Tucker Snipe.'

'This is rather weird.'

'Trust me, Gerry. Trust Tucker. All you do is hand this to the big man and get a definitive answer.'

Appropriately embossed from the PM's office, the handwritten envelope looks sound. I need anything now.

Parties and gatherings have always fascinated me. Wary decorum is how they commence, people stepping from the rain of hectic lives to steam niceties. Gradually – unless the hosts are vile, supplies run out or the place catches fire – they become microcosms, little societies with their own groupings and semblance of everlastingness. At Maria's with the possible exception of those poor locals for whom it must have resembled eternity the microcosmic era is soon reached. In the last phase guests break for words with ungreeted acquaintances, last-chance introduction to someone speculatively eyed, a final swipe at the drink. Arriving in immobile separation, guests part as motivated entities. As at a signal, my trio heel-swivels in different directions, business done.

Looking very Hampshire, my target is coming my way. I hang out my broadest smile for him to swim into. I know that without the envelope he would be unwaylayable and am inspired to say, 'Tucker Snipe'. And it works.

He is shorter than on television or in the public prints. That forelock which did so much for him when he pulled it at Conference, I am afraid that aerosol fixitives suggest themselves near-to. Quiff aside, his looks are ordinary except for the dark and predatory eyes.

'I should have known,' he says. Like a Commons answer, this gives nothing away.

Just a moment ago I was fondly hoping to clinch the match with a lucky boundary from however rustic a stroke; this feels more like lobbing the ball back from one's seat on the grass. As he slips it into his pocket, I remember Tom's scheme requires an answer for the PM; any such request is pinned in my throat by the genial ferocity of his eyes. All I have bobbing hopelessly in my mind is a scrap from one of

Cuthbert's 1793 entries: 'I could discover no ingredient of reply and so remained seated on my hands.'

With the unopened envelope he has snaffled the initiative. Speechless, I see Maria coming *arm in arm* with the other ruler of my evening. Hair-do flicking obeisance, he mutters something easy and correct. Maria whose eye for detail surpasses that of other women I know has 'picked up' the incident and her regard is slightly too maternal for my liking. Now the eyes of the Other put me in the shuddering shoes of some girl's first day assisting at Fortnum's or Harrods. The 'article required' is all too obviously within view behind his silk revers. Floor manager so to speak, he smilingly applies a pocket knife and scans the contents. 'An immoderate request,' he says. 'Rumour has a life of its own. I am asked here … There is a Junior Ministerial in my Department. Should it go to —' (he names the tartan terror). 'I always value the opinion of ladies when there is something to decide. Shall he have the job? How would you advise, Ma'am?'

'I have no knowledge of the person and no interest whatsoever in government posts. Dear Maria, as Gunther is bringing round the car, I shall simply slip off.'

'Not without I see you to the door.'

'Two minutes would be dazzling. I should like you to catch a glimpse of G. I am sorry to have failed the PM over housekeeping. Goodnight.'

'Ma'am.'

'And you. A shame we were so *inadequately* introduced.'

The black and particoloured sea is already dividing, its glinting eyes turned our way. Under any circumstance, Maria appears serene, but I can tell – I have seen it before but not previously of my doing. She lingers a moment in the politico's honeyed tones. 'Tucker Snipe,' he says, 'has never had such an outing. Made MI5 look like a limited company instead of the public liability it undoubtedly is.'

Maria's cool is arctic. 'Fascinating. Such a pity, Mr Arblet, we will not be discussing it on some future occasion.'

I say her name but doubt it leaves my lips. She is halfway across her room but further off than that from me.

'Sorry, old lad. Don't know what motivates you or who gives the retainer. Do know you're not cut out for it. You're not a pro. Whatever goose you were after, old son, on the evidence of the past five minutes, I'd say you've cooked it – good and proper.'

IN GOOD SEASON

AUGUST 1976

He is walking too fast for her on his long German legs. It had been her idea to walk there on her own, taking the map Uncle Charles possessed not much faith in. She had the compass Daddy had sent from America, oodles of holiday time and certainly enough French now to sort out left from right and right from straight on. But Uncle Charles had said …

'Not with all these abductions, Jenny. Your French peasant isn't above knocking off a nice little tourist. I'm sorry, girlie, but your mother would never forgive me. The country's in a funny state.' He continued doing something awful to his pipe. 'It was 1975, last year in fact with all that rioting in the Midi. We were down there, weren't we, K?'

Aunty Kate had nodded. She was doing something – complicated rather than awful – to a sundress and so had a mouth full of pins.

'I know we're in the bloody thing now, but I blame the Common Market. Sorry, Gerhard old chap, it's no reflection on either of us.' Uncle Charles let off a great blob of smoke. 'Saw the locals knocking the bung out from an Itie wine tanker. Talk about seeing red, the whole road was! Best place for the stuff probably. No, sorry Jenny. We shall all toddle over in the *voiture* tomorrow morning.'

On principle Jenny was fond of Uncle Charles – he was her mother's brother – but at the same time sometimes found it hard to believe how awful he could be without knowing it. Aunty Kate must have got used to him, or given up. 'Charles usually means well,' had been Mother's main defence when in the old days Daddy had passed the odd comment. Now Daddy was in South America with another woman and Uncle Charles was safer from criticism.

She was sixteen, generally sensible and self-reliant. From the hotel to the house was no more than ten kilometres. The idea had come from looking at the map. It would somehow make the place more special, more real to gain it on foot. An hour or two on her own! Jenny had seen that like an oasis, a green coolness of solitude where all the dried-out bits from the travel, from Paris, all the people who had talked to her in French and English, kindly meaning people: the dried-up bits could soak in that solitude and plump themselves full again. But Uncle Charles was in charge of things and Jenny could see beyond resentment now to make out the forms of adult responsibilities. Uncle Charles knew a lot of things and the funny state of France was one of them, not that she'd noticed it yet on this, her third visit. Mostly France was as it should be, the coffee smells, the little tables out in the sunshine ... the Terrible of course, illness, road accidents always happened out of the blue. Daddy's departure as well.

She would simply have to make do with half an hour before going up to her bedroom; there was a garden behind the hotel which would be safe enough probably. Aunt Kate had nodded off but must have removed the pins, not swallowed them. Uncle was awake over his boring old memoirs – Gerhard, he'd silently disappeared.

'I'm going to the garden for a bit,' she said.

'Take a turn before you turn in?'

'*Je pense que oui.*' Jenny was working on idiom.

'Jolly good. Don't be long.'

She left them to it. The hotel was an old one chosen by Uncle Charles because it was 'le Petit Bristol' and he had been born in Bristol; but as he had several times said – they could have done worse.

You got to the garden down a flight of wooden stairs painted blue, nothing in themselves but with a touch of elegance she continued to think despite avuncular warnings to guard against what he'd called 'total Froggification'. She did try not to think of the evening outside as *crépuscule*, it was twilight, but as French twilight it had a word no worse to describe the change from day to night. If you thought of words and things as a sort of mixture, as she realised she did herself. Mother had stayed behind in Dorset which was something to do with a gentleman friend. Nothing had been properly said and Aunt Kate, married to Charles, sailed under sealed orders. Relatives, thought weary Jenny, were in a class of their own. But then so were the people at school for example.

The Bristol's garden was big for its size with a pond in it, white park benches, and rocks genuinely sticking up out of the ground because this was the Dordogne which was proving rather a self-conscious area, geologically speaking. A positive cliff rose up at the bottom with one or two dark caves in it. You could imagine the night pumping itself out from these apertures. A silly fancy to turn the world inside-out, something you still clung to from being very small, like invented friends, like her dwarf, Ralph. Sitting on one of the frilly iron benches, Jenny could just once more catch a glimpse of him in the gloaming but distant now and rapidly dissolving in the coming night.

The future oozing from the present was forming an uncharted, shining lake.

But tomorrow, Jenny could picture that. The house would be of some interest, belonging as it did to Gerhard's French aunt. The Continental connexions were relatively abstract and nothing like the few but somehow absolute relatives at home. Yet 'people abroad' had been quite impressive at the end of term and beginning of holidays. She'd neither 'traded on' nor quite stamped out Sarah's making a thing of it, entirely in Jenny's favour. These days Jenny was wondering whether her intensely moral phase wasn't departing a bit, to follow the shorter and not so intense religious phase. God had never quite attained the solidity of Ralph and when she tried to project His shadow where Ralph's had been and where real shadows' deepening dowsed shape and colour even of fiery geranium, it was simply phony. Neither in feeling nor imagination was He to be conjured up, despite the declarations in the awful poem about 'a garden is a lovesome thing, God wot!' Uncle Charles went in for words like 'godwottery', 'airy-fairyness' and 'Froggification' – it was his style.

Dozens of people must have sat where she was sitting at dire or happy times in different seasons, different years. They were easier to have with her than God, though no more in evidence. Lovers meeting after years held apart by misunderstanding, parental ban, complex legal muddles were easiest. Danger of sloppiness there of course, as sternly agreed by the crowd at school referred to by her mother as 'Jenny's set', though Sarah's, if anyone's. It numbered about half a dozen and had unspoken rules such as jumping on 'slush' like tons of bricks. Odd how easily the bench, if you didn't guard against it, populated itself; odd to wonder what the others, even Sarah, were up to in the privacy of their heads beneath the publicity of hair whose main unspoken requirement in their group was to be unkempt as possible. Hers had become kempt in France and would not provoke a Miss Thompson accolade: 'Sarah' or 'Jenny' or 'Mary', 'you appear to have been dragged through a hedge backwards.' *(Traînée par une haie en arrière ...?)* Sarah was in Bournemouth, a town whose average age she had despondently declared was 105.

Feeling herself in danger of becoming a countess in an assignation with an impossibly romantic poet, Jenny got up to strong-mindedly examine the little pond for signs of acquatic life. She peered crouching into its opaque surface and saw only her face cusped by neat fair hair, a darkly mysterious version, burnished and somehow of the future. Jenny was studying the photographic effect and thinking about negatives when there was a cough, a scrape.

Gerhard's tall figure lay foreshortened on the slabby gleam. She scrambled to her feet.

'Narcissus I think did once that same thing and he happened to become a flower. Something like that.'

'I know all about it, thanks very much.'

'Excuse me,' said Gerhard. 'My uncle was asking of your welfare.'

'I'm fine. I was thinking.'

'Something nice I hope.'

'Oh, splendid.'

'Good. But I also have another thing to impart about tomorrow. I have said I will be your escort to the house.'

'You needn't. Thank you.'

'It is nice to start out very early, in good season. I have some fruit and a coffee flask. When shall I tell my uncle?'

'As soon as you like.'

'Oh, I see,' said Gerhard. 'I have meant to say the morning expedition.'

'Oh, I see,' said Jenny, wiping grassy hands on her jeans. 'Six.'

'I shall say to him it will be at six.' Gerhard's tallness turned abruptly but without heel click. He was very tall, thin, upright – and shy perhaps under his good English.

She could find no real annoyance at being caught on the hop, if kneeling by a darkening pond and staring at yourself *was* the hop. Had she been a frog, an actual not Uncle Charles one, instead of getting to her feet she might have hopped down through the watery mirror and into another world. The rage for frog/prince jokes so strong around Easter was odd to contemplate; some had been amazingly witty, but not one could she remember.

'Six' though had been a brainwave, being extremely early but not ridiculous. He had said something about August being best before breakfast and she thought that if that was pedantic or pompous then perhaps it had more to do with being a young man of twenty plus rather than being German. Unless he really was shy. Six though had to be got up to.

Jenny yawned experimentally. Yes, she was half-annoyed that he'd barged in to placate the Absolute Relative – and half-prepared to admit it had been thoughtful of him. She was half-asleep already with any luck.

He is walking too fast for her on his long German legs. Jenny decides to stop worrying about her suitcase which is unlikely to walk away from her room and unlikely to be overlooked when they open the door, any time now perhaps. Shorts, shirt, walking boots are all very suitable. The red silk square she has round her neck is there entirely in case the heat of the day comes early in these parts when it can go over her head to stop her brains from boiling, as Daddy once said back in her childhood. Very practical, the silk square and not at all to set off the light olive green of shirt and shorts. Practical too the compass in the shorts back pocket (she must remember not to sit on it), the four 20F notes in her breast pocket, the Swiss army knife clipped to her belt. The passport she has left behind in the hotel after momentary consideration, safer if kidnapped by a French peasant – she cannot feel much risk of that, unless Gerhard walks quite out of sight.

With one lingering waft from a *boulangerie* they cross the little river on a high bridge and leave the town to get on with its breakfast. He stops to wait for her.

'I go too quick for you? I am sorry but I was "miles away"!'

'Almost,' says Jenny. 'Kilometres anyway.'

'"Miles away" is correct for thought?'

Jenny teacher: 'It's idiom and means to be thinking of something else.'

'Well, I suppose so. My father was down here in these parts – with the *Wehrmacht* I'm afraid. I was thinking of him when he was about my age at that time.'

'Mine was much too young. Not that it's ever stopped him talking about his National Service in the RN.'

'He is in South America now I think?'

'Yes.'

'Are you fit?'

'Trust me,' says Jenny. 'As fiddle or trivet – no, that's "right as"; but I couldn't explain what a trivet is. I muddle it up with ferrets but I'm sure it's quite different. You know what a ferret is? It's a sort of polecat.'

'You are testing my English I think.'

'I'm quite a good walker,' says Jenny, 'it's just that I'm not particularly speedy. More *langsam* than *schnell*.'

Gerhard smiles for the first time since they all met up with him yesterday. It is transforming, like a door opening. 'Such excellent German, *Fräulein*.'

She's not quite sure how to take that – he is twenty, more than twenty, which (somehow allowing for mathematical processing as complex as calculus, if not like it a complete mystery, and taking into account factors of nationality, gender and being on holiday) makes him not so different in relation to her ridiculous sixteen as was Avril Hardiman who had taught first term before Christmas, stimulating adoration in Sarah's set – a beacon of what to become. 'The Young Boring English Cousin' has been her thought but – as Uncle Charles has said at least fifteen times since leaving Dover – 'What can't be cured, must be endured.' She increases her stride to keep in control the intervening distance. Gerhard is turning out better than when Mother first announced the whole astonishing plan and it had been *his* suggestion to lumber himself with this walk and her.

But being on one's own was so totally different from being with someone else. Walking by yourself, you thawed into a representative discoverer looking at the earth, a small universal – you between a few miles of air and a few thousands of rock. On your own you related to what you saw. Someone else even if it was mild, untalkative Gerhard: you saw things differently: you saw the other person and yourself large as earth and sky. You found the other world – theirs – sliding across what and how you saw. He was a step-cousin or something and his mother had married Aunt Kate's step-brother. A real maze! His father, young as him, here in the war was absolutely nothing to do with her but was now stringing along too! Perhaps he'd sat on last night's bench, calling a ma'am'selle *'Fräulein'*. Jenny sends him packing as quite *de trop* – back into the unbelievable past.

They are still on the road of ordinary black sort, if rather a small country one. Uncle Charles and Mother, come to that most middle-aged people at home, seem either to have funny prejudices about the Continent or else remember it from years back. Roads are one thing and sewage smells in towns which is a favourite topic of his – but, despite hot days and Jenny is sure a normal olfactory sense, she has not caught a whiff.

Gerhard is at the top of the rise looking at the map. 'We go here across country.'

'OK!' She feels the compass in her back pocket but decides to keep it for emergencies. The rocky, tree-shaded stretch with sounds of running water now gives over to wide landscape and the track before them is just a road with its jacket off. You can see enough to imagine a network of these sandy, pebbly tracks tying together the little farms and communes. One of Avril Hardiman's splendours in her short time with them was making some sense of Geography. This was an example of what she'd once explained which was that – unless interfered with by the meddlesome human intellect – everything would fit into resources at exactly the right interval. A lion, an anthill, a village: the next one would be found the right distance apart. Jenny is amazed how much she remembers or understands, more perhaps than she did at the time.

In the car coming down there had been a running commentary on the neglected and scruffy appearance of the countryside, but on foot it has its fine touches, an elegant carelessness like the Bristol's garden stair. Nice mixture of flowers growing in the cracks of sketchy, primitive walling, untended woodland (*boscage* perhaps?) – and suddenly a long thin strip of vines very neatly tended in the middle of nowhere presumably for some reason of the soil.

'We may stop for five minutes. Here.' Gerhard is getting two little bottles out of his knapsack. 'Orangina, good?'

'Thanks. It is a beautiful day.'

'It was a good idea, this walking.'

'You see more,' she says. 'More than from a car I mean.'

'Some days you can see everything.'

'I don't know about that.' To herself that sounds prim. To make up for it, Jenny jumps up to sit on the old watertank arrangement with wheels. 'You could I suppose if you were a bird,' she says. The metal, dinted and dark like the old pennies of childhood, is almost cold to her thigh.

'I shall sit also.' When he climbs on, the stolid object does not budge under the double weight. 'Water for the wines.'

'Vines.'

'Vater for the *Vines*. No, you could then see only what birds see. They have small fast lives and small fast thoughts. Do you not think that some days you can see more in the head? Everything, no perhaps not – more though. Bigger views of this life!'

'Yes.' Jenny thinks about the idea which is really not so different from her thoughts on being alone. Time ... and she now has an odd taste of the future, simply a foretaste of looking back on now, on sitting here; as if this was past and she remembered it. A slight shiver, not from the metal though.

Floating across ... *Pain-dur, Pain-dur* ... stale bread/seven slices doled out from a nearby unseen church. Oddly French, the double strokes. And it gets Gerhard down on his feet and ready to continue.

'Come.' Though his hand is outstretched, Jenny needs both of hers to get a little elevation in jumping off so as to protect the compass.

She stops herself explaining what after all was nothing – jump-offish, not stand-offish. But now he no longer strides ahead and they have fallen in step.

'We are all contingent,' he says. 'Is that the right word?'

'It is a word.'

'Incorrect perhaps. Time is hard, I mean to kick it off and be in freedom.'

'Perhaps it's an illusion.' Jenny is thinking of her father and that long letter he'd written to say it wasn't her fault.

'*L'existentialisme, c'est un arbre sans fruits.* It is a false idea to exist alone. But the past! All the parents. Oh, it is like this little sack on my back is full of lead or of plutonium which is heavier than lead.'

'I didn't know that.'

'From Pluto you know. I like the Ancient Greeks! Do you?'

'Ashamed to say,' says Jenny, 'they are not what I know about.'

'I have been at Delphi.'

'The Oracle.' Jenny's mind is thumbing blankly for more about oracles.

'I know my Uncle Charles is against the Common Market but it looks different to Germans with sacks of plutonium on their back. I tell you something else – the meaning of Delphi was to unify Ancient Greece and they did it as well by having a lady called the Sybil who always spoke a kind of ... gobbledegunk?'

'Gook.'

Gerhard laughs, the first time. 'That sort of thing. Wise men interpreted her words.'

'They'd have to be – wise I mean.'

'I don't know that. So Greece became a nation and by the year 2000,

Europe. Brussels is Delphi and makes gobbledegook, on paper this time. The thing we sat on, do you call it a "bowser"?'

'Yes.' Jenny knows herself better at words than Ancient History.

'Perhaps my father has brought it. I saw the little plate and it is an old German army one. War surplus and now it peacefully helps to make the *wines* out of the *vines* I think.'

'I shall be forty in the year 2000.'

'It has to be different by then.'

The hamlet containing the house they are to stay in (it belongs to Gerhard's Parisian aunt – this is a family which seems to cross frontiers) is called la Verteille and here is a small wooden pointer inset into the wall with the name on it! They solemnly shake hands. Jenny checks that her compass is safely pocketed. Now the track has a dip, a turn, a stretch stencilled by the shadows of small trees from which to burst into the first serious agriculture. At shoulder-height flanking their way: extraordinarily extended squares of a crop which is possibly, or will be, corn-on-the-cob.

Echoing Uncle Charles, Jenny hears his voice in hers. 'Common Market crop.'

'Soldiers.' Gerhard is right. These are regiments of grenadiers, the fuzz of the flower where the corn will grow mauveish in one regiment, more maroon in the other. Plumes in the headgear of the corn.

He says, 'It is most like Napoleon's *Grande Armée*.'

A little way further and, equally odd, equally paid for from Uncle Charles's pocket, *sunflowers*, great swathes again at shoulder level. But these have nothing military about them at this early hour; their heads are bowed and petals drooping. They share the same disposition, like the inclination of a crowd – mournful, distressed, a picture of lamentation. Coming so soon after the parade, it is more than an oddity to Jenny going along. It is almost a vision. Yes, these draggled myriads are a people in mourning!

She thinks to tell Gerhard how she has seen it but the moment passes. Too pretentious, too pat. But she stores the sight and its meaning.

He is now breathing deeply and swinging his arms. 'I do like the early summer mornings! I like walking with you! We are nearly at la Verteille. Is it perhaps American to say we shall be there in good season? We shall sit on the doormat and drink the good coffee I have. Somehow with this walking and with you, Jenny, as well – the load on my back is light as a feather!'

Older than any Common Market, a grove of wizened trees darkly aglow with small plums is before them.

'Look.' Jenny touches his arm. And inside this grove when you do look your eyes make out that what was just darkness between branches is full of birds.

'They are taking breakfast.' He speaks quietly but at their next step along the path the little orchard palpitates with wingbeats and then – miraculously, flock by flock – they all rise, head out in purposeful directions.

LIGHT

SEPTEMBER 1905

The light swells reluctantly, except that is a human word. Light has no choice and the reluctance is in those who must rise early and stop late in the toil of moving the world about. There are others, many others in this same town who will dawn to a different day with the sun almost ascended. This light supplies a September Monday, 1905, cloudless and beautiful all over England.

Before seven there is one – a charge hand on the tramway – stops off at the little pub on the corner of the street next to his, a little pub still known to the more philosophic workmen as 'the chapel of ease'. He stops for a scotch whisky, not because he has an undue liking for it, least of all so soon after a wad and cup of cha. No, it is because a friend of his has related a piece of advice from an Irish grandmother – whisky without an 'e' in it was what the good woman had tellingly specified. He is best described as one of those men you can see even these days in the corner seat of some ordinary boozer if you can find one, rather mournful and inoffensive, whose thin and restless expression on whatever size of face suggests an 'understanding of life' less far advanced than that of the rest of us; an expression which betokens a need to talk about it, if you're not careful. It was a phenomenon much commoner at the beginning of the century – the man, the expression, the bafflement in days when pubs and alehouses seldom had any air of pretension, in days when TB usually sheltered under a waistcoat.

There is a certain light perhaps peculiar to an English September more like dust than liquid, sprinkling any point it touches so that mean housing, flint facings, woodblock causeway – perfectly familiar sights – can gleam or, rather, dance a little. The pub in question stood and stands today (though in different use) off Church Street in the town of Brighton.

As the morning grew it was the sort of day, washday making it more so, to be outside, away from all the steam, the work and the martyrdom. Sitting on favourite kerbstones and working a pattern started long ago last summer with special worn-down penknives, they were discussing Royalty.

Porky said: 'How long you think the old Tom Cat's going to be at the wicket?'

It was a remark perfectly understood. For the third anniversary of King Teddy's Coronation there had been bunting, bands and all sorts. Even Brightonians on short commons who did not normally have matters of municipal prosperity on their minds seemed to know the town's dependence on a regular royal visitor from each generation since Prinny built the Pavilion.

'Not so long nor his ma anyway,' said Adele.

The two boys scraped at the criss-cross design which is still there today observed by the observant, but unexplained; they all contemplated the possibility.

'Na, he's older to start off with. About the same age she were when she kicked the bucket.' Drake, king of knucklestones, was scraping with his left hand whilst practising the stones on his right. Watching his hands made you wonder at him.

'Pull the other one, why don'tcher?' Two years older than the boys, Adele was used to being outspoken to a streetful of urchins. 'She'd have to've had him before she were about ten year old in that case and that aint in the nature of things.'

'There was Sarah Grainger,' said Porky who never liked giving in without a fight and who always supported Drake because that was how they both got through – by helping each other. 'She tried it and it killed her off.'

'She were more'n ten,' said Adele. 'Fourteen, something like that. Usedter do skipping with her. Poor Sarah. Blooming terrible shame to get caught out that early. Won't catch me having kids. Sleep in yer own bed and say prayers every night. It's not a world to bring more mouths into.'

'I dunno.' Porky had a considering side to him which sometimes he wished he didn't have. Nothing you could be definite about, nor ask for in a shop like a ha'p'orth of salt for Mr Bates to saw off the block with a blade that left its rust; just something you knew you had like your other habits. Some folk never questioned how they went on, never thought about it. Drake didn't. Which was why he was king of knucklestones. 'There's good things in it,' Porky said.

'Good things such as?' Then Adele relented; she usually did. 'There's sunsets and that. What I like is going down the Front when it's chocker. What I don't like is people toffing yer.'

'Don't take no notice then.'

'*Don't*,' said Adele. 'Good as la-di-dah, me, any day of the week.'

'Old Man went birdnapping yesterday. Sold ten larks to the Metropole. He's up on the Downs again today.' Drake – and it was a thing Porky liked in him – was capable of making the odd conversational effort.

'Up with the skylark, was he? Ours is still sleeping off his Saturday night, so think yourself lucky, young sir. Lark-eating's as toffing a thing as you'll get. Not a proper mouthful in it – finicky food for finicky folk.' She watched the knives scritch-scratching on the glistening stone. All she had previously got from them when she'd asked its meaning was a dunno; the pattern was something they had started and got on with, like washday except with no purpose.

Adele knew that her mother let her off washday in an effort to make up for the man in their house, her own father she was sure, despite stories. Listen to stories and you'd never know anything for certain, not that you did know much. You knew your mother wanted the best for you to redeem her own life – not that she was a complaining woman. Looks was something, Adele supposed, and she'd got them from her ma, not that she knew anyone they'd done a blind bit of good for. But it was the reason she felt every bit as good as la-di-dah, if you got to the bottom of it. Porky was thoughtful, Drake harmless and there was worse places to be sitting on a day like this with the old street looking its best, if it came to looks. No one in the end could tell much about your life. Mrs Lochrie's tealeaf-reading had been an excitement but only yesterday Adele had overheard Mr Grainger telling someone that Mrs Lochrie was 'sick unto death'. Holy Bible talk always gave you the shivers, though it wasn't unknown just to open it and stab down your finger in search of a sign.

'Back to Central, school again next week for you lot,' she said.

'Blooming gaol,' said Drake.

Porky said, 'I like that new Mr Cross. He said this is a new century and every year we'll get higher up in it and have more of a view. Told us about climbing mountains, didn't he?'

'He's alright,' agreed Drake.

'He said more you know about things, more you climb out of shadow. He said one day you'd get such an eyeful that you'd run down and tell the others.'

'Stood on his desk,' said Drake.

'He climbed on the desk,' said Porky. 'Bet you never saw a teacher climb up on the desk, didyer?'

'Women's got more sense. Last year before leaving was best. They called her Miss Woods – masses of red hair and Irish blood. You must've seed her.'

'Rides a safety?'

'That's her. Name of Daisy and all. Walking out so she'll be needing a bicycle made for two, shouldn't wonder. Not mind that much if I *was* going back to Central. She'll be left herself though if she gets spliced. Funny innit, Monday's the only one in the week when I don't stink of fish. Spent weeks dreaming they said things to me when I cut their heads off.'

'Fishes?'

'*That* daft and it was mostly herrings. When I started Mr White who's a good old feller told me about a woman who usedter come in for a dozen fish heads to make soup out of to strengthen her brains. Every Tuesday it cost her fourpence. After some weeks she come in and arst him what a dozen herring might cost her and he told her eightpence. So she says to him that way she can still have her soup and a couple of fish dinners as well. Harry White told me he says to her, "It's working, missus, it's working." He's alright but I dunno – think I'll go into service at the end of the chapter. If I hear of a decent berth.'

'I'm for joining the Royal Navy,' said Drake, 'just as soon as I'm let.'

'He's got the name for it,' said Porky.

'World's your oyster sort of style. Never did know why they say that. You can call Cheeseman's toff but Gran usedter say oysters was common food and me, I'd as lief have a swaller of seawater. Here's Sidney coming.'

The street contains about thirty households and knows the adjacent streets and the riddled courts between. It knows how to get on one of the new trams if needs be to go to work or Rottingdean. Even some of the women whose husbands hold down regular jobs are adventurous enough now to go on the rails. Streets differ and everyone has an idea of the character of different streets which has more to do with the people there than with amenity. Your own street has fewer mice and rats (ingenious and ingeniously disputed theories as to the reasons), or – if more mice and rats – why then a better view or bigger front rooms. In the end, however broad-minded, big-hearted, well-disposed you are, you can never quite understand how people can abide to live in some street other than yours. You get on with what the world has given you and it's a streetful of everything. The Graingers, and Sidney is one, possess romance and tragedy to a considerable degree. The mother was drowned off the West Pier as part of the Royal Jubilee celebrations of '97. Father was left with Sarah aged seven and Sidney not yet five. Mr Grainger was perfect for the part – hardworking, a drooping moustache, heartbroken and a tendency to Consumption. For years the street had rallied round. Sarah's demise in very premature childbirth was therefore much more a sorrow than a scandal and there was probably no one from the street in whatever state of inebriation or moral certainty who would not, should anyone *not* from the street be ill-advised enough to animadvert to the subject, suppress it by a fist, a look, a sneer or a snort.

'Pull up a slaving pab, Sidney, and sit down.'

'Thank you, Adele. I've been stuck inside reading.'

'What's it about this time? Ancient Egg-wiped, I'll be bound.'

'You'd be out of date then. Ancient Greece, but they did overlap.'

'Ancient something anyway,' she said, 'tell us about it.'

'Might as well,' said Porky.

'I don't know much yet.' Sidney Grainger was felt by the street to be a scholar, which not every street had. It nursed hopes of him. He was thin but not rickety, pale but not pasty and was capable of the most beautiful expressions of face. Something in him sometimes came out like the sun. Because of his tragically interesting background half a dozen of the street's best had mothered him. 'I suppose,' he said, 'that Ancient Greece might have been a bit like now on a morning like this. With sunlight I mean, because they had it most of the time down there and they built with marble, not always, quite a lot. Like stone blotting paper blotting up the light. I don't really know how to say their names: Plato is easiest.'

'Know about him,' said Porky.

'Remember that Prof Plato on the Palace Pier, electric kite flyer?' Drake with a magic deftness in his hands appreciated anything like it in another. He had always been good at climbing along under the main deck, undercutting turnstiles to witness in the free fellowship of art the amazing acts of the various Professors each summer drawn into town and then to where the town dabbled its toes, on one of the piers.

'They thought of the human mind like the sun. Plato did as well – only he had this other idea that everything we see or feel or think is like a smudgy copy of what it could be. He calls it Ideal Forms. I've not worked it out, but if you try and do anything like draw a picture you know it's not as good as it could be. So it might be like that somehow.'

'Sounds a long way round the houses,' said Adele.

'It does,' said Sid. 'But I don't know if it is.'

The four of them sat contemplating the infinite possibility of things. Drake and Porky carved away at the old design. It had been Sidney's idea in the first place and come from something he'd read on the Phoenicians when an assistant at the Public Library now grandly formed out of part of Prinny's stables (an assistant who knew more things than the Corporation's rules he was employed to follow) had let him sneak in under the flap. The design was a mark for them to gather round on warm, free days: their special stretch of kerb in their special street.

The reprinted sunlight of Edwardian scenes has become common enough now in all the popular topographical books. Your eye must have peered closely at the smudgy presences of ladies along the Front or of urchins in the slum streets – all those cut-down waistcoats, jackets, large caps, pinafore dresses, unisex black boots probably with holes in them. And if you have seen three dark-clad smudges sitting with a light one on a kerb by the roadway with a caption commenting on how little traffic there was 'circa 1900s' – I have told you who they were.

OTHER STORIES

DRIVING HOME

'Logarithms.' The word lingered, the last heard spoken as he made his way out of the place and towards the car. Though what Jack Delancey knew about mathematics! Now he was enclosed, surging – and the pent-up power there under the bonnet was like a caged beast. There was respect for it, sheer respect. Life was a zoo sometimes: tigers but mostly the chattering monkeys, comic exhibits; oh yes, the occasional giraffe. Jack Delancey, what about him? *Logarithms*. A baboon all right. In spite of all those natty clothes, because of, all you saw was his hands, two pounds of sausages not of the cocktail persuasion; and his massive head, a crude job rough-welded out of cast iron. He slowed up a bit to keep within the speed limit. Could afford to.

Now that head, that skull. How thick was old Delancey's skull? A millimetre, ten millimetres? How thick are skulls? Jacko's was an object all right – you saw it was an object, most people's you didn't. People *were* objects though, when you came to think of it. They built these great buildings, bigger objects than they were – but people were objects! Small ones. The brains of Einstein or a filmstar's breasts would go into a briefcase.

Lights.

The brakes stopped him quickly and the springing dispersed the weight, speed, mass of his motor car. 'Not for town work though.' Prentice's opinion and startlingly original like all Prentice's opinions. How Prentice got on the Board was one of the seven wonders of the world, the eighth. Sir Frank of course knew his man: Prentice was a simple device, press the button and the light went on. Admirable move in fact on Sir Frank's part with that Hughes faction all the whispering was about. Sir Frank was the driving force. Business needed that. 'Town work' though! Why didn't Prentice accept his simple function without all this pretending that he meant anything at all in any real sense? Prentice with only the one directorship probably had less take-home pay than he did and doubtless a tiny 'family saloon'. Not surprising he talked of town work then. In fact it was typical of his thinking. Anything bigger than was strictly 'necessary', anything with reserve, with extra, was not suitable. *If I'm small enough, they'll let me park.*

Glance up; lights on green.

But that *peep-peep* was insolence. Up the gears with the speed of reflex. 70 mph in 10.5 secs if you wanted it. With acceleration like that you could afford not to jump the lights. He remembered that small drivers were always out to score and he felt better. It was someone like Prentice behind him, or Prentice himself. *Peep-peep*. He swung back to the line: 30. No police about and hardly anyone else: this city died at night. But that was the point about responsible citizenship – you were your own police. Otherwise a 50/50 ratio would be necessary, totalling more than 25,000,000 in the case of Great Britain. It almost was, the way things were going.

Empty town, a strange seashore. The tide was out. It left its litter, its tiny erosions. A great tide of feet. How many thousand human tons over one paving stone? Along here he had come in the over-warm afternoon which had caught most people out unsuitably attired in overcoats and raincoats. Legs impeded, there were too many layers of cloth over you, trapping you in with the heat and dust. Struggling as part of the rush, you saw your own reflection jumping in and out on you – shopwindow, door, shopwindow, door.

Matches! Several places went by. Public houses on the point of closing, garages still open and probably selling matches, went by – for the motion of driving stopped you from stopping. Perched in a car like Prentice's stopping would be no problem; but in a seat designed to make you part of the machine you could go on indefinitely. Matches though. The city was running out and the road promised only a district of neither one thing nor the other before the decent suburbs started. But not much hope of getting matches there.

Brakes! Almost an emergency stop.

He got out into an acrid wind and immediately a filthy newspaper tendrilled round his leg. He entered the place kicking at it and manual removal was necessary as it had followed him in. He fed it to the wind and went over the mat – ƎMOƆ⅃ƎM – entering backwards.

'Care-*ful*.'

A girl had collided with him, thin and lower class, really a mop, frayed played-out peroxide mophead, coffee in hand.

'I'm terribly sorry.'

'Ah'm terrahbly surry.'

A vile-looking specimen at one of the tables said that – with a black leather jacket and black teeth and seemed something to do with the girl. Brute indifference was written all over his face. It was pointless to take any notice of him or of any of the others slouching around. The decor he did register, a crude yellow and blue washable wallpaper copied at tenth hand from the style of real places like the Bentinck Grill. Behind the counter all was scruffy and unhygienic with every sort of public authority simultaneously indicted. He said to the old harridan: 'Have you a box of matches?'

'Freppenorfippenny?'

'I beg your pardon?'

'Ah bigg yooer pahdong.' A crass giggling squelched behind him. He kept his temper – a power in reserve. For his inspection the old crow produced a box of Swan Vestas and a threepenny box.

'The Swans,' he said.

'The dickybirds.' Rubbish-tip wit hitting its peak. It annoyed him to find he had nothing smaller than half-a-crown. Almost for a certainty the old hag would have to go upstairs or next door for change, exposing him still further. She did not however and he took his matches, his money and his departure.

'Goodnight,' they chorused, 'goodnight, goodnight.'

He lit a Stuyvesant, switched on and revved the engine. The power to some extent burned the distasteful scene away.

Some germs needed 2,000 degrees of heat to kill them off. Set a flame-thrower of tremendous power at the door refining its heat to effect a purification. See the long-thrown tongue first darting behind that counter, the foul and stale foodstuffs gone without trace or trouble, the harridan rendered into fat of great clarity, the matches producing their tiny flames in welcome. The decor licks effortlessly away. The mop-head girl translates into a fiery wand and the criminal youth perhaps ... fries a little inside his studded carapace.

He did not linger. The road was wide and straight and he would soon reel in the miles, have a decent drink in his hand, put on a disc – *South Pacific* if he felt like it – have music.

By the turning he was going so fast he almost overshot. The narrow, familiar, bending road was darker though still day: a summer dusk heavy as lead.

Summer trees overstraddled the road. Call it a road – lane almost, country lane. Slap a coat of tarmac on a cart track and think it suitable for this day and age. Not that he didn't like the rural approach himself sometimes. This time of year there was a sort of weariness about nightfall, as if the earth had trouble getting off to sleep. Weary earth.

Everything was made worse, exaggerated by the sort of day it had been. Thunderprone, almost chilly at times but making you sweat. Even the car seemed to labour on bends round barns, beneath the huge exhausted trees. And people were definitely affected – machines then which responded to atmospheric pressure differentials. A machine which would never have its efficiency impaired was difficult to imagine; but they were aiming at that, aiming at the moon – a fact. Human engineering was at a primitive stage. Pinstripe pressure suits, he smiled. But such an invention would smooth business and have made the evening at the Bentinck a degree, a millibar more bearable; kept Prentice and Delancey on a more even keel and – he now admitted it – have helped him better to put up with them. And would Society, let alone Business, ever function efficiently, with total efficiency? Those café louts – no amount of pressure (or pressurising) would get *them* to adjust. Sand in the works was an old-fashioned phrase now when even a speck of dust, a misplaced molecule threatened the machinery, but ... sand in the works all the same. And it was appropriate because Society was still at the stage of low efficiency yield like the steam engine. Nothing short of purification by flame, he thought despondently, would flush the system clean of such residues.

A place where the road was suddenly nipped by farm buildings heralded the straightest stretch. By the clock on the dash he saw that it was later than he'd thought, almost night in earnest. He accelerated through and was soon on 60. He knew the road. At the end of his vision he saw something: lights quested it, shooting their smart tongues on full beam. Motor bike or scooter? He closed on it rapidly. Scooter it was. And then the road betrayed him, throttling itself almost dead between high banks. Throwing away speed, he knew he had missed his chance. If only he had concentrated more further back, or had added a few mph coming out of town! He hung on its tail and inspected it.

For a few seconds its rider seemed to be the criminal youth of the café – but it was physically impossible. One of the same sort right enough. Dipped headlights showed him all he wanted to see. Black jacket with sequins (PETE – some missing), long lank hair and – significantly – an L plate horizontal on the pannier. There was nervous back-glancing: a learner plainly enough, despite the attempted disguise. It was also apparent that he was thrashing his machine as if not to be passed. On the crown of the highway and not doing 40! Overtaking was impossible – on this stretch oncoming vehicles had to stop, then edge by.

What else? That hair – no crash helmet needless to say – it floated in the tepid breeze, almost a foot long. Fancies himself a knight in armour among his barnyard hens. But not wearing a crash helmet – sheer folly. How many surgeon-hours were spent picking through bits of skull shatter, patching up his like? Unless his skull was on the Delancey pattern, he thought, relaxing a little. It would be a long wait.

Where the road reached absolute zero of width the youth waved him on. Incredible! The equivalent of the café insolence. There was something radically wrong with Society's laws to allow this sort of thing on the roads. Communication – he seized on the idea – was crucial to the smooth running of anything. Clear the lines of communication and provide free access for the necessary driving force and you were halfway to your goal. This bloody young moron was doing his bit to foul things up. Leaving aside his probable failure to hold a current provisional driving licence and be in possession of the road fund licence certificate, you still had other flagrant visible failures. No crash helmet; unprominently displayed L plate; the sort of hair which could bring a factory to a halt and endanger other lives; and – as a bonus – an improper hand signal. Not to mention the buzzing sight of him trapped behind the windscreen. He was in the way of *South Pacific* and a decent drink.

Over a slightly humped bridge he knew that the road widened for a few seconds; the scooter was doing 38 according to his own speedometer which was a feature and as accurate as anything on a production model. His eye checked over hair, leather nazi-type jacket, concealed L plate in one final concentrated glance. He applied acceleration.

The scooter touched his front wing gently and seemed to strike the grassy bank before coming back hard for more near his rear wing. For a fraction of a second, a molecule of time, he thought he was going nose on into a field gatepost but lightning reaction plus immediate mechanical response got him through and for many seconds he concentrated on the clean speed of the unimpeded road. Bloody fool, he thought, and it was settled there and then. No crash helmet – he was asking for it.

Hadn't he said so? He remembered quite clearly that he had.

BEAUTY

There was a strange bit of charm about the place, he decided, braking with care on the cobbles. What charm was – dismounting to ride in on one pedal ... imponderable, but not one of the verities – coasting up to a blackened wall a little too smartly and taking a flange of skin from his knuckle. Like a stage-set perhaps? Finding his padlock, forgetting his pain. It was all simplified now into surprising colours. Dennis got the chain round and firmly on the hasp. His lock, American and a thing of rivetted plates fit for Fort Knox, was one to trust in. He stood, bike secure, a last minute to himself.

Yes, that scrap of canal was now a masterstroke. The Fruit Warehouse old and black, the Bonded newer, blackening – had dingy windows plated with fire by a sun which laminated wall and angle with violet shadow. The darkening mean railway yards functioned as contrast. This beauty was an apple of his eye, unintended in the building, unheeded by any save the precious few. Precious, 'precious' ... Dennis's ideas of Art School, of himself as an artist welled strongly. Beauty was fitful and odd in the world of the city, or else only fitfully seen at odd moments. But it existed, seen or not.

Night which comes from the sky seemed to rise from the cobbles of the ramp. Dennis stooped to hook off his cycle clips and someone from his first day as a casual worker last week was right there behind him.

'What a oppertunity! Yo ter get down S Yard smartish, Mr Riddle said. Clocked in, ent yer?'

'Not yet,' said Dennis. 'It's not nine.'

Copper said: 'Get a double shuffle on and get down S.' Copper shuffling on himself, ill co-ordinated; Copper trying to strike the fear of God – kicked like a sack all his years and looking for a sack to kick. Certain things needed no learning such as the simple mystery of Copper. Dennis dumped it and crossed to the Time Shack which said so in faded, almost Roman lettering so that he half-saw there an emblem of our faintly inscribed abode in the universe. Copper was left-righting into the distance. The men did not much like Copper but, judging him harmless, buried their dislike as a point of etiquette. When Dennis had punched his card even the clock agreed him to be four minutes early, proving it had not been only speed of imagination flying him through nightrise and dayfall – the observed and stirring universe which so strangely escaped the older men. Pulling the lever stamped you with the simple justice of the clock.

S Yard was the place of overtime, hard graft and story. It was Parkinson Street's front line, its holy of holies, and if anywhere deserved the meanly flowering obscenities S Yard was that place. Dennis started out for it; he was a little nervous of this world and happy when he could to escape to bright petals far from the black root. Last week the Yards had remained rumoured territory as he had steadily got to know the Sheds. The whereabouts were becoming obscure here and Dennis saw himself wandering for half the shift. Perhaps Copper had got it wrong and he should have covered himself by reporting in the normal way to the dusty office where Mr Riddle sat, often in bowler hat, bombed out by years but Authority still.

A large waggon (from Italy by the wording on it) stood at the end of its journey – and of its days by all appearances – another country's Parkinson Street had yielded it but as exotic here, he thought with a shiver, as a wilting Camellia once adorning the bosom of the South. A small brick hut had lights and Dennis half-jumped from rail to rail towards it. The warehouses staining into night impressed now by hiding, not revealing, their massive shapes.

He who both suffered and soared high above being seventeen approached the hut in a twofold spirit, both as 'the lad' and as something else stooping from afar. That things were simultaneously ordinary and extraordinary he knew in his blood.

The door was open and they were all in there: Len the ganger was smoking his pipe, Irish Mike was exploring his first snap. Blaggers was there. Blaggers looked up.

'Look what's blown in. Been on the nest?'

Copper's stupidity saved him. 'Yo can tell by their eyes.'

'Lot you know,' Blaggers said mildly. 'Come on your bicycle?'

'Yes, my old bike,' said Dennis.

Len stirred himself. 'The time has come to see what lies in store for us.'

Good-humoured, foul-mouthed guessing concluded with the last word going to Rickert, the little Scotsman: 'Eight hundred tins of salmons' eyes to tickle the palate of the local nobility.'

Last week Rickert – proving that object of interest, a reader – had produced several books for Dennis to look over. These, mostly from the English Language Publishing House in Moscow, were translations of Lenin, Stalin and others but, instead of exoticism, had reminded him of nothing so much as Aunt May's slabcake, old dread of childhood and qualm of present day.

Albert, who kept pretty closely to himself, said: 'What about them London youths, Len?'

'Mr Riddle didn't commit himself,' said Len.

This caused amusement. Parrish spoke. 'Jimmy Riddle by name and nature. Couldn't commit his mother to marriage, him.'

'He's nae so bad,' said Rickert. 'Give a man his due. He sees through what he's doing. Petit bourgeois maybe, but the man's no idea of himself as a tyrant.'

'Him with his bloody godlessness and his maniac atheist Stalin!' Irish Mike's snap was a neatly folded bit of greaseproof now. 'I'll be in the stands, Jock, at your Cup Final to see how your blether goes down with St Peter.'

'Preferred to your repentance.'

'Repentance, is it? Stuff that.'

'Confession – it's the same difference.'

'Is not, then!'

'Well,' said Len, the Englishman with pipe to prove it, 'if we get stuck in I dare say there'll be an hour or two's kip for later on. There's bunks in the staff waggon.'

Blaggers said: 'I sleep in my own pit and no bleeder's else.' There were utterances of Blaggers no one followed up.

After Sunday's sweet forgetfulness Dennis was once more taking his mental notes. Blaggers, as black-browed and terrible as his name, stated something difficult to grasp.

'Give them Londoners two minutes,' said Len.

'Give us a roll,' said Mike.

Rickert dab-handed some Old Holborn and they all watched his fingers as they might have watched Chopin's. When Irish Mike was alight they were beginning to dismiss the very idea of Londoners. Yet all last week there had been talk of them. Twice Mr Riddle had told Len that he'd got him Londoners. 'There's a pair of Londoners coming I could put on.' Sad words like a small case of canned fruit hitting the deck. All last week! Beginning his second week, Dennis could look back to that far first day when Mr Riddle had handed him over as 'the new lad', an arrival perhaps proclaimed for seven days previously with 'I'll get you a lad.' So this Monday Londoners might emerge, though Mike, who had perhaps been thinking similar thoughts, shook his great head and murmured 'London's not your man.'

Manual work: references to it at school and home had been slight rather than slighting. It was what people did if they didn't 'have brains',

brains being prized (if not excessively) – preferred certainly. Failing brains, there were hands to pick up a bit of money with, and pocket money if you were a student. In manual work your brain had merely the importance of the hand switching on the Dictaphone, dialling numbers in mental work.

During his first week Dennis had pondered manual work whilst doing it. Unskilled labour did not ennoble the doer as in one Victorian painting he had seen reproduced – a roadworks dominated by a navvy whose eye pitched Olympian distances further than his shovel – but you were changed and this not so much by being reduced by others to the status of a 'hand', not by your honorary membership of the lowest of the low, but more simply because inside was turned out: your body became you. And though there were differences between, say, Mike's musculature and Rickert's wiriness the gang did not give them attention. Rickert, Mike, Evans, Parrish, Blaggers – even Copper, even himself – all were curiously equal before the task. A common body emptied trucks or loaded drays, sweated or swore, received injury ... As far as Dennis could see.

Len fished out an envelope from his shirt and slit it neatly with a little finger. 'Bloody hell.' From Len's tidy life they drew their unity; from Len mild swearing boded all sorts. 'It's grain in sacks!'

Dennis perched on this information, not knowing it worse than cans in cases or the bottles of disinfectant he had smashed on Thursday night. 'Washing the deck?' someone had said.

'Grainstore?' Blaggers was darker but deeper tonight.

'That's right.'

They found the waggons after a bit, half a dozen standing by themselves.

'Old stock,' Dennis felt entitled to comment.

'Built nineteen-canteen,' said Parrish.

Len told Dennis it was experimental grain from Scotland. It was pleasing to have the confidence.

With seals struck off the head waggon, they couldn't open the doors. Three pulling on each made only inches. There was a discussion over whether to go on to the next one or beat the problem first. It was a discussion, though more like baulked animals who turned and sniffed, Dennis thought, including himself. It was up to Len, and Dennis was pleased to have guessed the decision a second before Len said, 'We'll do this perisher first.'

Such was order and the gang was happy.

It meant the drag. The oily wire rope was located between the metals; someone in the Sheds was dug from his sleep to start up the donkey. But it was twenty minutes before the slack went, the strain took and the waggon door shot clear out like a time-punched card. Now darkness involved warehouses and sky, the Yard lights tinkered with the shackled earth and you yawned in sympathy with pillowed sleepings.

Each hand bogey took three sacks, two horizontally against the end iron and one upright to steady them. For fifty yards you staggered a plank road to where the elevator of the Grainstore took you for a brief rest – then along a corridor to snug wooden rooms as warm as the insides of a haystack; then lightly back to step on as the next arrival wheeled off. Back chilly but swift to the waggons. Half a dozen such journeys had you refusing to be beaten. So the railway truck again with Mike perching another for you to embrace, its weight all you could hold. Wrestler or dancer, you invented deftness and sometimes the waistless maiden fell into place, sometimes redistributed her shapelessness so as to fall off halfway to the elevator. Three times it had happened and Dennis, down for the count, hailed it with fists and obscenities and got it there with white rage. Rickert hung back as he came down and changed barrows with him wordlessly. The new one had side holds and rubber tyres and saved him so that he graduated from relief to confident mastery and when Len said in passing, 'Break now or do the third?', he said, 'Let's do the third.' The third waggon contained different grain in smaller sacks, five to a load, more amenable and also, because it went straight in by the ground-floor entrance, quicker without the hoist.

It was nearly one o'clock in the morning when they jacked it in, arranging themselves Roman-fashion around walls built in other days of wood and craft. Normally food was not shared but tonight Len produced a whole bag of oranges; Evans offered his Woodbines round; they shared the fatigue.

'Funny old spot this,' said Len. 'God knows when they built it but Mr Riddle reckons it a wonder. It's got three walls inside each other and ducts to move the air round. It's like a good concert hall is good for sound. Latest ones cost thousands and aren't better even with compressors and God knows what. It's living grain and it needs air and warmth like the rest of us.'

'It's a bugger alright,' Parrish said – a sort of agreement.

'It's warm.' Blaggers did not bring sandwiches and had been the only one to refuse Len's orange. 'Unnatural.'

'It's natural,' said Len.

'It's bleeding warm.' Copper.

'Bit like the middle of a hayrick,' admitted Len. 'Grain gets internally combusted sometimes.'

'Internally combusted!' The phrase took.

'That right?'

Addressed, Dennis nodded, adding something about hayboxes, doubting he knew much, concluding lamely ' ... so if you leave it long enough the stuff cooks.'

'It'd rot the food,' said Blaggers.

'I don't think it takes that long!'

'I'd not eat it.'

'I must admit I haven't.'

'There you are then.'

'That's right,' said Copper.

'Internal combustion.' Parrish shook his head. 'Yo a student, youth?'

'I suppose I am.'

'Not studying religion or owt like that?'

'Not particularly,' said Dennis. He had no wish to bring up the subject of Art though half-thought it would be all the same to them: Learning, a mystery they accepted in its old medieval entirety.

'Remember Arthur?'

'Heavy specs on him,' said Irish Mike.

'He wor a theology student and us effing and blinding,' said Parrish. 'We were never so fucking embarrassed.'

'Each sack,' said Len, 'will be a field of blooming wheat.'

This surprising comment seemed to please all though Rickert was probably biding his time to pronounce on agricultural wages and Blaggers, well Blaggers either worked or sat still – one or the other; never smoked nor ate in company; sat, hands resting on knees, blackest of Buddhas. 'There's plenty on the side down in Lincs.'

'It's a money economy, comrade, and you're telling me they pay in spuds.'

Blaggers laughed and then said: 'In Lincs they have their sisters.'

Then Mike gave the signal to go by shifting and then rubbing his eyes. Only he of all of them improved throughout a shift and now Dennis returned to a theory of the previous week that Mike – like sheepdog or other working animal – had been bred to the task of moving the world about. This theory was slenderly based on a confidence of Mike's that his father had worked on the Mersey Tunnel and that his grandad had driven spikes in Oregon. Yet animals were bred by choice of human will and Dennis without religion believed in the individual soul.

'A pair of waggons,' Mike rubbed great hands, 'then lay down my blessed head.'

Rickert said: 'Don't break your halo.'

'Dinna fash yersen, Jock.' Mike rose with a glittering yawn. 'It's Above so it is, waitin for me to slip it on.'

The fourth truck yielded a new monotony. Dennis's thoughts of temporal brevity and length fitted to the nature of this work. Great pencils of the Masters caught a minute to catch Time out and land the everlasting moment. Over several trips his mind wheeled such airy sacks to store. And tiredness was an acceptable gift of life. Passing Mike, he grinned back, all theory falling through the ground: he knew Mike through body more than mind.

Rickert had hurt his foot right up on top of the elevator and Len had put him on marshalling the trolleys, nearest thing to light duties. Such news got through.

'How is the foot?'

'Nae so bad. Gives way now and then because of a bit of fascist shrapnel, lad, before your time.' Rickert smiled. 'Soon be done.' His face was struck as if by sunlight, a look remembering his younger self.

Dennis now felt fatigue filling his muscles. Poor dogsbody was waiting for the word which he would not give until Len gave it. The final waggon was a ragbag with remnant sacks of all three sorts mixed together and with Len to sort it. It meant a mixture of journeys – elevator or ground-floor rooms. A word from Len and off you went to the appropriate destination as in dim childhood he had once played buses in a boarding-house garden with a boy called Ken. He was on an elevator run driving a tin green sixty-seater with Polaroid vista windows. The dark shapes of the warehouses reminded him of his arrival on shift hours ago, the pictures suggested by simple colour and form, something beyond those, some feeling of moment ... If he could do it, be an artist! Statement without idea, the capture of beauty ...

And the fiery sun seemed to be returning as he had seen it, a range of windows kindling his imagination. The sun was returning to set in the middle of the night. It glittered on the tracks, it washed wall and corner with lambent strokes. Blaggers ran back, agitated. Len ran across with the others following him from the last waggon. They were all there, except for Rickert. Fire unfolded their senses. They thought slowly. There came a baffled dash, flapped back.

He appeared at the top of the elevator, strangely dark against the radiance, but you could see his arms, legs and head. They shouted. It was hard to see if he moved or stood still. It gathered itself, though Dennis saw it only later. So it was that happenings overtook time.

He could have been crying out in panic or saluting them in some fashion: they could not tell. Afterwards these things are reconstructed and tell the tale they must. Blaggers said, 'Poor bastard' – that he remembered.

He could not remember ... exactly, thinking back. It was too difficult

– a figure against the flame. The flame. The memory was not clear. For a long time there was a thought of painting it but that did not seem right, seemed morbid. Had Mike wept? They had gone at it like baffled animals even when the firemen came – quickly. Dennis thought of Rickert caught there like a torch – but it was difficult. He put it indefinitely aside but it remained there.

TRIPTYCH

'Owe my life to that dog.' The dog in question continued pooling its energies in deep snooze. Larry looked from Jennifer to the man and then to the dog. How she took things, how she reacted – he needed to know all that. She had on her bright expectant look. Jenny could spin out a lager and lime indefinitely but he said, 'Another, Jen?'

Larry took the man's pint glass and his half through to the bar, there to be replenished in the careful Scottish way. You almost expected to be asked payment in the funny old money. 'Two shillings' it still said on many 10p's. A place like this was from before the Flood. Worlds slowly changed into other ones, like cells of your body; after seven years you were someone else perhaps.

'Got ye in tow, you and the lassie,' said the old character, whatever that meant. The arithmetic was done on a sort of barrel organ which shot out its drawer with a ping. But prices are always up-to-date: £1.40. 'It's all trade, y'ken. Yon rents his spot on the bench with blether.'

'Is that the poet then?' Larry's good eyes had gone to a little portrait print with the single word *Burns* beneath.

'Aye.' The barman unhooked and gave it across.

'Genuine.' Larry could tell that from the faintly mottled paper. Feeling an all-round expert, he added, '"A man's a man for all that."'

'Y'ken eleven children on the wrong side of the blanket and dead before forty.' The old man chuckled and put the poet back. 'But yon in there's seven days a week.' Larry made private eyebrows.

The man and dog and Jen were all where he had left them. She gave him a greeting smile, how proprietorial he wondered? He landed the beers. She approved of generosity, unlike narrow-fisted Joyce.

'Here's to both of you,' said the man. 'And to the Age of Opportunity! The age you are,' he explained. 'Governments are all guff. When I was fourteen I stowed away on a balloon.'

'A balloon?'

'Yes, young lady. It was Northants; not what you'd call the Judea of 1934. Flowing with dole queues, yes. Flowing with milk and honey, no.'

'What sort of balloon,' Larry asked.

116

'Gas, the property of Captain Charles Hendrix – no more "Captain" than I was at the time.'

'Go on,' said Larry.

'It was town gas. And that was how I did it. Ragged-arsed kid, if you'll forgive the expression – one of about a hundred. I held the coupling from the gasometer and when the balloon was stuffed to the jowls I hopped into the basket. A hundred feet up before he noticed and rising fast.'

'What on earth did he say?' Jenny's attention minted gold.

'"Bother me", or words to that effect. No one but Hendrix anyway would have ascended with a nor'easter blowing forty knots.'

'Did it blow you to Brighton then?'

'This young man of yours has brains. It did – in a record time.'

'What about your parents?' she wanted to know.

'Both of them died in the Asian flu of 1919.'

'You were *orphaned*?'

'Not a month old.'

'Who brought you up?'

The man took a strong final pull over the brim. 'Who didn't?'

'Poor little you.'

'Let me fill you up.' This time through in the bar Larry found his money taken in grim silence. Had he given offence? It was just that with characters like this the gap was Stone Age. Jen was still on about being orphaned and he was telling her about the orphanage. 'Biggest in Northants with a thousand kids in fifteen dormitories which must make it nearly one hundred kids per room. Great doom of a place. It may have been because Northants is central, clearing house sort of style. I cleared off all right.'

'Were there house mothers?'

'It was more like the Roman army.'

'Captain Hendrix,' Larry asked, 'did you stay with him after the balloon?'

'Year or more. Turned out nearest to a parent I had. He was one who made a lot out of a little. He was a conjuror.'

Jen said, 'Rabbits and hats!'

'Hats out of newspapers, bless you. Newspaper headlines out of sneezing! The wonder of the 1930s. Do you know what I learned?'

They shook their heads; the dog was cushioning his massively on Larry's shoe. 'People don't believe in themselves and would rather believe in anything else.'

The revelation hung for their inspection. Was it true?

'We brought Astrology to the West Country – Gloucester, Chepstow,

Malvern – toured the lot. The Red Van Men. He'd a Rolls Royce built up into a van – simple but brilliant. People are usually too dead to enjoy travelling in a Rolls Royce. We cocked a snook and gave folk a leg up at the same time. That's what never fails. Same mixture of patter and concern as the medical trade. I was Sorcerer's Apprentice – fifty years ago.'

'Isn't there something about not altering a Roller?' Larry was recalling his time as student of *Vintage Motor*. 'Some document you have to sign if you ever buy one?'

A strong voice said: 'Get *him* to sign anything at all, I'll buy you a drink.' The man had a porkpie hat and blond eyebrows, a man to say what he chose. 'He's an institution or is it that he ought to be in one? More free drinks than a fish, more lives than a cat.' The man turned his large bottom at them and resumed talking EEC subsidies.

Their man ruminated quietly. 'Some of us have needed more lives than a cat.'

'Such an awful start though,' said Jen.

'Human nature,' their man said. Nothing followed. There was a menu on the windowsill. 'I'm having salad,' she brightly declared.

'Should have been a caterpillar,' Larry explained.

'Chips and chips; you wouldn't think he'd ever seen a colour supplement!'

A girl had slipped through the forest of backs; their companion ordered steak, Jenny her salad and Larry had gone in for the cheap pastie when the waitress warned him off it. 'Weekend old. You're in a skinflint place.' This she said to Jen. Men's and women's business, there might still be something in it.

Going for more drink, he was pleased Jenny had nodded a second half. The old character took for the food and nearly cleaned Larry out. His face was dyspepsia. Taking the pitifully small change, Larry pleased himself by saying 'Rennies' as in a foreign tongue which has words to say 'thank you' for people's thanks. Back in the room, the dog which had saved his master's life was on hindlegs, forepaws on table and tongue excavating the small remainder from the pint glass. As with most dogs, it looked simultaneously pleased and surprised at its present position.

'He's over eighteen,' Jenny explained. ' A dog's year is seven or six and he's four – so it's all right.'

'Arithmetic's not her strong point.' Larry had noticed himself establishing her with comments.

The porkpie man said: 'And hygiene is not this one's strong point.'

'Sorry?' Larry was still on his feet and thus on the other's level.

'Keeping things germ-free,' said the confident face. 'Know about dogs?'

'Sort of,' said Larry.

'Half their time with tongues up other dogs' bums.'

'They sniff each other,' Larry conceded.

'They do more than bloody sniff. I could be drinking out of that jar tonight.'

'They wash the glasses out, don't they?'

'Is that so?' The man emitted more than forty years of disbelief.

'What's that about?' Jenny wanted to know.

'Search me.'

Their companion was silent as if he had shot his bolt, or as if meeting in the then-uncrowded pub had allowed spread wings and a sniff at a life less earthbound than EEC subsidies. His hair, still black but interfered with grey, had once been sheeny. He was unpreened.

They were all hungry, even Jenny and her lettuce. The dog was politeness itself in consuming one of Larry's three sausages. 'Thanks, kids,' said the man. 'I shan't forget.' It was time for their bus. They shook hands and the life-saving dog extended his paw.

In holding the door for her, Larry planted a kiss of love near her ear. Crusty and unpredictable to the last, the landlord opened the streetdoor for them. 'Central America this time? Or was it the frigate HMS *Amethyst*?'

They left the old unbeliever. Larry's pocket had enough coins for the bus, his hand guessed.

The sky was tall and silkenly festooned.

※

Slowly the old man levered himself down to sit, which had not been the purpose, first bus and then walk, of his journey. Just to sit! It was such a carry-on these days to get about. He could still do it and that was more than could be said for any number he could name.

It was a surprising place for him to be taking his ease. Likely he had fettled this bench, or were they new now? One good thing, the little wind sweeping round the park was warm enough to pass even Madge's muster. An up-and-down place, this park – always had been. Steep by name and steep by nature. Seen old Alderman Steep once; must have been much younger than he was now. Some of the temperatures they had worked in, some of the days! With work to be getting on with, you don't sit but when sitting becomes work ... then you have to put your backside into it.

MONTHS

One way or the other, He keeps you busy, He does that!

The reason for coming out was to get a new angle on things, on living there and burdening the daughter-in-law. Like that wireless chap once said – 'You gotta have an angle!' The burden for her increased with the old age. One thing though, it's Madge the one he's sorry for; but he'd never believed in rattling about Number One. Practice time for St Peter come at last. Come the Day, they always used to say, you'd have to account for yourself to God, or else to St Peter. More probably it would be some trainee saint you'd never heard of, like half the Royal Family these days. You had to have something ready in case you got called out unexpected; just like school or in the army. Who you got up at the Golden Gates would most likely depend on the size of the intake. Even though folk didn't die so much now there was twice the number of them. You'd be lucky to get some lance-jack angel.

'Don't you go tiring yourself,' had been Madge's last words at the bus. Things women said. With a woman you listened, with a man you had to believe there might be some sense in it first. Tiring yourself, my stars! She had meant it for the best. The sun falling across his hand lit the still-golden hairs there. The back of your hand was what you were supposed to know so well. Miss Winthrop at school, turned by Time into the bonny lass she was, would always say: 'Class, this you must come to know just like the back of your hand.'

He'd never thought much about it. He turned it over. The palm was St Peter's territory where the young looked for love, success, a long life. A long life he was having still; love, never enough of that. So ignorant they had all been.

Gardening was the line his life had followed. Mr McTaggart was visible again as the solid, bristly self he was in the jungly light of the Corporation Main Bedding House. The six of them holding up bedding rakes for his inspection! The trouble Mother had out of that blue apron, sometimes almost spitting venom onto the flat-iron. To be under Mr McTaggart's eye was next best to being a plant and you got the same shrewd looking-over. Well, life on earth was only a place to set roots for the flower of your immortal soul. Gardening and military, they were opposites really. Mr McTaggart had some RSM in him though! He'd served out his own time on a ducal estate, which they never heard the last of. But in the end Mr McTaggart had been a fine man, never knowingly unkind, good both inside and out. Between them Miss Winship and Mr McTaggart had taught him his writing and arithmetic, his gardening. Bright flowers of memory! White blouse and gold chain, the hairy forearms.

Thumbing-in, pruning, building walls, this park was properly more his than Alderman Steep's. But Madge kept you so much on the hop – even in that bit of a potting-shed – that you could never form your plan. All intended for the best but you had to get away to look at it from her angle! She tidied you until you couldn't think.

The sun lingered in the tiny forest of his hand but not so brightly now. Nothing ever stood still; tidying was just Madge's wish to keep things so and an old man was harder than a cup to rinse and put back. No matter how he bit his tongue he could never become as uncomplaining as a cup. There had been big changes for her in the year of 'the arrangement'; Jenny had been there first off, part of the household. Grand girl, granddaughter. He'd always see the crouching four-year-old watching him set plants, hands on knees, big eyes. Good for everyone, Jenny had not been a fixture. It was a vacation or something and then next minute she got her degree and was off with young Larry. That was how it had started – in the dazzle of Jenny around and the cocoon of work and worry which mothers and daughters make for each other. At the start he had moved freely from the bustle downstairs up to his room which had easily swallowed up the contents of his long-widowed home and then perhaps down to the garden which still had plenty of work left in it.

Such good youngsters! To believe the half of what was in the papers you'd have to stretch your mind, assuming you had one to begin with. Young Jenny was a warm thought to have in the world. According to the papers there were now eleven rotten apples in every dozen; sense told you different, there was one as there always had been. Life grew the knowledge in you and you came to recognise times for taking up, times for letting go. This seat, he now realised, was not his work. It wasn't properly set and would have rocked under any man of more than his skin and bone; any courting couple worth the name would have had it arse over tip in ten minutes. Fifteen years now since he'd hung up his hat. Now the whole notion of work seemed to have gone daft, or gone.

Jenny left home probably for good, Joe off working in the Middle East: Joe and Madge in their mid-forties already. Husband away was the trouble. It was obvious now. Joe was due back inside the month and that gave time. Always it had been an odd feature in his life how, once he had made up his mind, something came along. Down the Club with Joe, stuck up alongside someone at the bar, you got into conversation – no one without a tale to tell. Luck though to have had his ancient union card when the young chap turned out to be a full-time officer. Had wanted to tape-record him; there were fewer every year who'd been through the General Strike. If it hadn't been for Mr McTaggart, who knows, he might have been on the dole throughout the whole of the Thirties.

Now that he had made his decision, unless he got on with getting up, he'd be dead in the park like that poor devil before the war. With Joe's return Madge would be needing more of his room than his company and must be given no chance of saying different. The young trades union chap had said to ring any time. Brush off the soil for his tape-recorder and sign on for the Rest Home, two birds with one phone call. A feeling of manhood told him it was right. Then Joe and Madge could get on with their lives. It was never more than even-stevens for anyone on earth. He was pleased to see it so clear, tickled as well that forty years of union dues would be paying off.

The Home was south somewhere according to the young chap. He was on his feet without thinking. This was the time for rooks and rheumatics to come home to roost. He looked finally at the park. Rest Home, quick march. He imagined it as an army billet complete with bedpacks and full of men waiting to be posted and he saw himself entering in, the same man as ever.

※

'It makes a change.' It was the umpteenth time she had said that.

Joe unfolded the deckchair for his wife. 'Get the weight off your feet,' he said.

'Not where the weight is,' said Madge.

'Can't have you skinny.'

'Not skinny, but ... you know.' She sat with some attempt at the old gracefulness. Little things were what hooked you in the first place, half-noticed ways of doing things. Everyone had dozens but only love noticed. Joe felt unexpectedly expansive. 'It's a change for me too – only cooler in my case. Not that we didn't have the use of a good pool out there, we did.'

'You sent a picture.'

'Olympic standard, the pool not us. Chalky White fixed up a race one time.'

'That one you brought home.'

'Yes. Expats versus locals. Hard to say who won when they wouldn't follow the rules.'

'That's not much good then.' Madge was fiddling with the parasol arrangement.

'Let me do that.'

'Thanks, Joe, thanks a lot.' She sank into the puddle of shadow, kicked sandals off. 'It's nice to get away.'

He was dissatisfied and couldn't find any reason for it. Marriages went stale in the nature of things and maybe he was still half-attached to the expatriate life of the past months, who could say? No picnic but it had been money, and more than money. A simplicity of life in the 'accommodations'; Chalky and that funny Frenchman, Pierre-Luc. Then there had been the work and some first-class Heath-Robinson when UK had shipped not the right part but the one you had to make right. Only Chalky and he would ever know what went into those valve-linkages. Chalky had engineering brains and it was a pleasure to work with a man like that.

'Fuengirola,' Madge remarked, 'it's a funny old name for a town.'

'Could be Arabic.'

'Arabs on the brain is what you've got. Spain's Europe, isn't it?'

'This place could be Blackpool.'

'Don't be daft. It's much nicer.'

His dissatisfaction was boundless: airports, skies. You could end up not believing in anything. He knew himself for a sensible man however. Arriving at one LHR terminal, stashing kit, meeting Madge after months, then straight out on another jet was a turn-round in any book. Return was never easy anyway. Chalky was the world-expert on that: two of his had ended in divorces. Not one to do things by halves, old Chalky. He missed him. He was missing and also missing missing women and missing missing booze. Madge had spread a bit, no doubting it; the complexion she was guarding, well it had been mottled by the UK climate. He was fitter than he had ever been – lean, sunned, strong. Time not distance made the heart grow fonder: she was still Madge and mother of their daughter.

'Never quite fathomed the Arab attitude to women,' he confided.

'I should hope not.'

'It's repressive over there.'

'I don't think Jen would run around like that, do you?'

That was a couple of girls going by with a shriek of English and no costume tops. 'Not if she was an Arab, she wouldn't. All wrapped up in black and hardly visible. A bit like my old Gran really – my Old Man's mam.'

'I never got to meet her as you well know. Not because she'd died off or lost her marbles. Because she couldn't be bothered.'

'Dad said she put her energies into reaching ninety and had no time for anything else.' Joe knew the comfortable moves of this particular conversation.

His wife sighed. 'Must have let her guard slip then or else worn herself out feeding the cat. Three months short, wasn't it? Prince Charles's eleventh birthday.'

'Don't know how you remember that. Now dad's best part of eighty. What was that you were saying on the plane?'

'He's gone and signed himself into a Home.'

'I thought he was staying with us, all fixed.'

'Not good enough for him I suppose.'

Joe said nothing. The sort of thing the Old Man would do; could be he had only moved in to keep Madge company. Him gone, Jen left and his little bit of property sitting there as yet unvisited. He could just do with poking round it now with a nice spot of English rain coming on.

'He has done the garden a treat, I must say that.'

'There's a bit of a breeze,' said Joe. 'What say we walk along a bit? Here's like a bit of downtown Manhattan.'

'There's the towels to think of.'

'Hotel name all over them. Safe as houses. Get an appetite for dinner.'

'It's full-board and they do steak and chips.'

'No foreign muck for you, eh?'

'You can't be too sure where it came from.' Madge clipped her handbag.

'Used to be a walker, didn't you?'

'Used to be all sorts,' she said.

The sand was firm underfoot. Joe knew his wife capable of talking herself into a state; stopping that happening was one of the tasks he had forgotten about; but now she was more of a challenge to his feelings than to once-accustomed mental reaction. 'You still are – lots of things,' he said. But it was difficult to tell if she was mollified. Near the sea the breeze was nicely razoring the edge off the morning heat. Yesterday had been the courtesy tour which had taken in Marbella where filmstars could be sighted, though Madge's Sean Connery had been denied by the Scotswomen on the back seat. And Gibraltar had been glimpsed in the far distance looking like the jade elephant, he thought fondly, on the mantelpiece of childhood. Perhaps the Old Man would take it with him into the Home. From here the elephant was hiding behind the flat sea.

This Costa del Sol was building faster than Kuwait; from the bus he had noticed a skinny flock of sheep with neckbells trying to graze the narrow plots between villas. They'd go to feed expat pets, dachshunds likely. Krauts and Brits were all over. You had to hand it to the builders though: draw out the foundations in the scrub like a magic circle and hey presto! up went the breeze-block and they covered it like

Hollywood. God alone knew about mains services. The magic circle was money. Join its madness to people's half-baked dreams ... bearded weirdo's were wasting their time all right.

They had reached where the raked beach had become scrub with dumper tyremarks. Crossing that, they gained a little stretch of dunes. The dunes were knitted together with some sort of cactus plant, squatly showing off violet flowers. 'Hey,' he said. 'Remember Skeggy? If this stuff grew back home you'd have come back with more than love-bites to show your mates.'

'I don't know how you can!' she said. She was pleased.

Then they came upon one of the houses which had been here before. It waited, semi-wrecked, for destruction. You could tell that all the new ones tumbling off the backs of mixer lorries had been modelled on it. Yet it was quite different. The front door gaped but the stairs looked safe enough. Madge did not know if they ought – but they did. They stood together at first-floor level. The window doors were thrown back and caved-in but the balcony still had the protection of a railing of wizened iron. From the height they had gained they could just make out the continent of Africa.

DREAM

A year after she died my aunt seems to have left me a sort of keepsake, every night for more than a week now. Which is why I am telling you about it.

I'd never expected anything. All she had (which was the house really) went to Norman who sold it of course. Norman is in Insurance in Slough and the one and only thing special about Norman was his dad shot down in the war before he was born. It's a distinction which has worn off by now. But, draped in hushed tones, his dad's was the picture standing on the silent piano. 'That's your late Uncle George.' He'd been caught in RAF uniform looking exactly as if he knew that his first trip as air-gunner was destined to be for keeps. No, she didn't leave me Uncle George who must probably be in Slough, face-down in a cardboard box. Not fair when I don't know the first thing about Norman's wife, and *that's* not true either: she's called Elspeth. No kids I've heard of and so perhaps she hangs up the ancestors for family. Didn't get to the wedding in 1970, though I was asked. Norman, well I could claim to know him but the years go by and perhaps people change.

When she died a year ago I not unnaturally raked round for memories of her. Not much came back. She was a well-meaning woman, I'm sure of that, and I must have been a trial to cope with at the time. I was for myself. For boys like I was, aunts rate with the furniture. Norman was – still is – a couple of years my junior and all we had in common was our mutual recognition of the burden of being dumped on each other's hands, the sort of perception kids are good at. Incompatible adults on a desert island would take a year to develop that then-immediately-formed odd bond. Why desert islands have always been big news to children is maybe because in some respects that is what childhood is.

I almost sunk myself with the profundity of that statement, DIY Sartre, if you've heard of him. Think it was him who said that Hell was other people. That didn't fit my aunt's case and besides, unless they were family or the meter-reader, other people didn't enter into it: the front door I mean. Hell could have been widowhood, or could have been me. I used to come at irregular intervals like migraine. The reason for these attacks was my parents' marriage; they went in for years of rows and separations starting as early as 1945. At the end of Hostilities, hostilities commenced. One up for Sartre you may be thinking but oddly enough they finally settled together for a golden old age. But that's another story.

This one needs a bit of getting back to. You have to realise that my visits happened without warning and, more often than not, without toothbrush. One time, acting with the collusion of an usherette, my mother yanked me out of the Saturday rush, in the middle of the film. Here I should list its title, stars etc. and claim never to have found out how it ended. I'm not here to fool you by making things up; about that film I haven't a clue. For me my aunt's house became a sort of sword of Damocles which must have been the way the poor woman viewed me. No, her house was not so much like that legendary dangling object, it was more like being attached to it by elastic: a dull home base to which I would suddenly and unreasonably be snapped. The official family home in its varying abode was unsettling and alarming, but also exciting. Hers was a backwater or – to stretch metaphorical wings – a Sargasso Sea.

She was worthier by far than either of my lot. Whereas they sacrificed plates, wedding vows, household pets, me; she sacrificed herself. She was somehow suspended between my uncle's fiery death and the coming of television, a gap to be filled with making jam. Much was talked of 'Kilner jars' in those days and doing everything in its season; brand names were nowhere much except for 'Tizer, the appetiser.' Looking back, you imbibed the notion that the world was pretty well fixed. My aunt got on with the jam and kept the world out of our hair; I can remember that she was amazingly grateful once when I helped her with the Kilner rubber rings. As this is in a sort of filial – nepotistic surely cannot be right – vein, I ought to add that she never mentioned haircuts as my father did (not all the time, but at terrible intervals). Were haircuts men's Kilner jars? Civilisation then was closer to the Minoan than to today's ways of going on.

I ought now to get on to the dream which seems to come from her as a legacy, not that she features in it. Does it draw its substance from what secretly interested her? Is there more to it even than that? I have this feeling that her involvement is like a satellite beaming it into my dormant head. First I must tell you a little more about what you have already pictured for yourself. Her house was on an absolute suburban street built by white-feather men in the early Twenties for heroes to live in. Small in scale, now I come to think of it, that street was a seedbed for what came to be 'normal, ordinary' English life. As soon as it went up that street must have filled with newly-weds making use of the new hire-purchase plan (small down-payment and then a tiny weekly sum); I see them laying lawns and paying milkmen, starting families. There it suddenly was, a set world but always more live-and-let-live than keeping up with the Joneses, let alone the Clagworth-Joneses. Next door was almost certain to be doing the same thing and so your curiosity was mild. I understood none of this at the time. In the ever-hot summer deckchairs would be set up on handkerchief lawns, handkerchieves spread over paternal faces to shield them from the face of Father Sun. The Home Service brought Cricket or else Wimbledon through each french window to swell into a street-long harmony.

Only one house told a different story. Here the thin gossip of the street drew to a focus and burning-point. This house literally stopped my aunt's street dead, making it a close or, more accurately, a closed street. This fine distinction is of some importance in that the street resumed with the same name after the blockage – Campion Street, in actuality another close. The odd property snipped it in two but I can't remember a name, nor imagine it could have had a number. Why it was there I can only guess at – history and the law's quiddities, manorial court leats for all I know. It was not from antiquity, no Tudor cottage. It mocked the mock-Tudor of Campion Street by a very small seniority of years, just as effectively as children do. A period gem would have stood no chance with the builders. The history of things is always getting lost but I do know that the Mr Clagworth-Jones I knew had inherited it from his father and builders would have stood very little chance against any block he was a chip of. So perhaps the old block had done in Campion Street's ideal ordinariness and sat there in the middle, affronting both halves at once.

There were stories and rumours around of course which, as was usual in those days, tended to be fed on speculation about the war which still stood in heaps between then and the sunny land of *before*. It was typical that much of this rumour festooned the mighty head and shoulders of Clagworth-Jones. Some said he had been a Conshie spending six months in the Tower of London – or the Isle of Man. He had been an interpreter for Lord Wavell, a boffin in Wales, a submarine commander. These options all gleamed with possibility. I am surprised now that I apply myself to the task, how much detail I picked up without knowing, from things said by my aunt perhaps. The man who read the gas was Mr Shaw who always took a cup of tea and, fresh from the Clagworth-Jonesian meter, had a sort of authority. Mr Shaw was of the opinion that it had been cloak-and-dagger work and

DREAM

when Ian Fleming years later opened the bag to let out the first of the hundreds of mangy cats to scavenge the rubbish-tip of our national imagination, well, I'd been prepared for it by Mr Shaw in Campion Street.

How oblivious was the man himself to all this interest, did he know and was he amused by it? What do you ever know of being discussed behind your back? It was just long enough after the war for people to start looking back on that shattering mountain of event; adults were a population slowly thawing out. I should also tell you that Mrs Clagworth-Jones had an independent, if smaller fame. Called Prunella for a start, she was suspected of having been an actress, a ballet dancer (I once scored cheap approval by ungallantly commenting on her size). My aunt tended towards the opera theory – her identification was Prunella Mason, based I think on an early *Radio Times* found lining a drawer. Another mystery never cleared up. I recall my aunt's very words: 'She looks like a contralto. You can always tell.' Her words took weight from her piano playing, not that she ever practised once George had taken up his eternal residence on top of the instrument.

To look at, the Clagworth-Joneses were unlike the average denizen of Campion Street. For a start was size. We carry a belief that the first Elizabethans were miniscule types, whereas if you ever go into one of the more fashionable London pubs you will observe how much the young have shot up to bang their heads on the ceiling of this century. Search me what the average height was immediately postwar. They towered, she tapering from her singer's helping of bust; he wide all the way down – high-coloured, hugely bearded. Beards then, unless on the Player's fag packet, were a public-order offence.

This is how the dream begins.

I have wandered down my aunt's stump of street one summer evening. Time stretches linen-thin and the hour in prospect is no way different from a year, a day, a week. You know how a fading suburban evening can depress you at the best of times; rising fifteen is not one of them. I can see him up a stepladder clipping his hedge, not the regulation short back and sides, not in the least. I stop, trying to puzzle it out.

'Hello, young shaver,' he says.

'What is it?' I cannot fathom out how, him with his back to me and me in plimsols, he can have even known I was there.

'A work in progress,' he says and looks down at me as jovial as a bear up a sapling. 'Daft thing to say,' he goes on. 'It's going to be Adam or else Eve, depending how the chest comes out. I hope this one will be Eve – not created in the right order but there's more to go at on this side, if you see what I mean. Besides, creating Eve is more fun.'

'I see,' I say.

'If I do it,' he says, 'that will make my garden Eden. You know about Adam and Eve, don't you?'

'"Went down to the river to bathe",' I foolishly say.

He laughs. 'And Pinchme. Who told you that?'

'My aunt.'

'I thought so. Had to do something with all this foliage and so I thought of Adam and Eve.'

'Will you do clothes?'

'That's the point, old man – they came into the world starkers like everyone else. I see what you're driving at. Surely not though? Causing offence sort of thing? I'm causing a hedge if it comes to that. Do you really think so?'

I shuffle. 'Dunno.'

'Not offensive to you, eh?' He climbs down. 'Come in and have something whistle-wetting winkled out for you by Prunella. Sarsparilla, lemonade. Tizer is not unknown.' Near to, he is hugeness itself, a mighty man. 'The old place is not what most folk would call tidy. What do you think of the lawn?'

'Could do with a haircut,' I mumble.

He shouts a laugh. 'Spot on! This way.'

We next round the corner of his dwelling. I have never seen such an extraordinary collection of objects. There is an old horse-van on knock-kneed wheels with resident chickens; a model of the Eiffel Tower tall as I am and painted red. A shed with a sign on its door – DANGER over skull and crossbones on tin: a notice from the war perhaps. On top of this shed sit a row of concrete owls and in front of it stands a very odd contraption indeed with a seat and engine but no sign of wheels. 'That,' he says, seeing my interest, 'is probably an idea going nowhere, not even fast. Isn't your aunt thinking of buying a vacuum cleaner?'

'I've just got here.'

'Damned expensive and hard to get hold of one but they're interesting. How's your science? Sorry, no intention of nagging you about school subjects. It's just that by the laws of Physics everything has an equal reactive force. A vacuum cleaner sort of sticks to the floor by sucking in. Now if it blew out it might sort of *hover* off the ground. What some insects do on ponds with surface tension. Not quite, but it gives you the idea. If you could create your own surface tension then you could scud about with minimum resistance. Don't suppose I shall ever develop it, but the idea's right. Sure it is.'

'Pond skaters,' I say.

'Those chaps, yes.' In those days people like Mr Clagworth-Jones said things like that. Sometimes but decreasingly as the old people get 'replaced' you hear such archaic phrases on trains. It comforts me; fewer and fewer of us went through the war. 'You know, old son,' he says, 'the pond skater is the fellow to imitate. Shan't get off the ground myself, not now – anymore than poor old *Mayfly* there, Prunella's name for Hubby's Folly Mark Umpteen. Go-getters create their own lift with gift of the gab and so on. They jump sideways and you find them in Parliament, sideways again and there they are running British European Airways or Imperial Chemicals. If you want to get ahead, forget about a hat: get yourself a cushion of air and *scoot.*'

We are now at the back of the bungalow which has a veranda round most of it. Mr Clagworth-Jones rushes the last few yards, moving sideways and stops inches from crashing into the glass door. He makes a grunting noise, returns to me and this time advances with a sidling movement and arms half spread. The door opens before he gets to it. 'Photo-electric cell, amazing little thing. It needs a lot of bulk to make it work at this stage of development. Come on.' He takes my arm and together we step through into the veranda. Inside there are wicker chairs, plants and an Indian canoe suspended from the roof. 'This is my place for thinking in,' he announces. 'Do you get ideas?'

This sets me back a bit. 'I think so.'

'Topping answer! *Cogito ergo sum* is Latin meaning that the thinking bit, the cerebellum, tells us we're here. It should have another cog put in: I think therefore I *think* I am. That got missed out. Come and meet Prunella and sip the fabled liquids. It's through here.'

I wipe my feet on what looks to be a fairly ordinary doormat and he laughs out one of his impressive squalls. 'It won't bite you!'

The kitchen is cool and dark and ruled by a woman's hand. She comes from another room, large but moving with female neatness through the world. She smiles. The Clagworth-Joneses are large but not sinister.

'This young shaver,' he explains, 'found me clipping away at the infang. He's been on the tour of inspection and quite rightly found the lawn in need of a haircut. He now requires liquid refreshment.'

'Sit down at least,' she says. 'What would you like? We are not used to boys.'

'Tizer,' he says, 'would do us nicely.'

'*You* I am used to. He is whom I'm asking.'

'Yes, please,' I say. 'I've had it quite often.'

'One thing led to another really. Showed him the poor old *Mayfly* – that's Prunella's name for my brainchild by the way. Technically, it's the C-J Self-Elevating Vehicle prototype. You'd think with Export Drive that Mr Attlee would take an interest. Well, you'd better have another think coming in that case. Finally, Pru, we got thinking about how people get on in the world.'

'That,' his wife says, 'will really be the day. Not that I haven't known quite a few successful people. I have but rather a while ago.'

'This one has it all before him. That's probably why I went on a bit.'

'No, I'm not blaming you, Dearest – really I'm not.' It is a tenderness I have never heard before and is almost more memorable than the rest of it. 'He is not a Spiv,' she says to me.

I say: 'Some of those things were pretty spiffy though!'

'People are polite to me in the queues,' she says. 'But I sometimes wonder. Probably they're thinking nothing of the kind. Everyone has a heightened idea of his own importance, even *her* own if she hasn't been *completely* downtrodden. It's inevitable we have such an idea when we are with ourselves twenty-four hours a day, except for sleep.'

'I know!' I am warming to her. 'My aunt takes an interest in you. You're probably quite famous in Campion Street.'

'I'll fetch the fizzy.' She gets up. 'And we can drink to fame and fortune all round.'

'Does your aunt say … much about us?' he asks when we are alone.

I shake my head. 'I just come now and then really. Usually I'm living closer in – to Town I mean.'

'Didn't lose your father, did you?'

'Good heavens, no!' I say. 'He's all right.'

'Quite a few kids did though, these last few years. Or sometimes it's the other way round. Prunella is a good sort, you know. Tell me about school.'

To my own surprise I tell him. He has no need to know and yet has asked the question straight. If ever my aunt asks it is only because she thinks she ought to, or sometimes perhaps a wish to be of use; she went on about name tags once. My parents never ask because their energies are in their private war which leaves me out. This mild, whiskery enquiry from Mr Clagworth-Jones launches the possibilities of my school life like a great ship to the sea, a contained world in the palm of the sea, in my hand, to describe. I tell him of buildings full of stairs, the botanical rock garden kept by Mr Trickett, an angry old man who is both deaf and dumb, of Miss Cook our form teacher and the last female left on the staff from the wartime arrangements, soon to be given marching orders. I say, 'She's all right for a woman,' but not that she has saved my bacon on at least two occasions. To see it whole and tell it is strangely releasing. He puts in the occasional prompting question and then takes a tobacco pipe from the drawer. 'Grow my own from seed behind the workshop. Prunella's not too keen but then I think she's gone to the Service Stores for the Tizer. When it's light they stay open late.' His pipe flares out a smell like all the bonfires of autumn and layers of cloud which (because we happen to be doing Meteorology in Geog) I happen to know is strato-cumulo-nimbus.

'I could have sworn that you lost your father.'

I freeze in the knowledge that I was right all the time about grown-ups not being dependable. My ship is over the horizon. I see myself terribly. He sits under clouds at his kitchen table.

'Here we are.' Mrs Clagworth-Jones places a shopping bag on it. 'Comestibles including Tizer. Ran into your aunt on the way and she said it was OK for you to stay a bit but to send you back when the shadows lengthen.'

'That they do all the time,' her husband says.

'Do you know what a pessimist is?'

'Sort of.' Now I do not like the way they question, not that they use any nasty or sneering voice; the way I am pinned by their little askings.

'*He* is a pessimist, my good man there. What your dear aunt simply meant was shadows lengthening in any evening. At other times they don't.'

'Do you play chess?' He has found a couple of chess things in that drawer, a horse and another – I don't know the names. 'Chess is the oldest game in the world.'

'The oldest with rules.' Prunella unloads her shopping – a loaf, a half-pint of milk, the Tizer – except it's ice-cream soda. 'Mind your p's and q's,' she says, tidying his chess things.

'Norman's dad was shot down,' I say. 'That was *Norman's* father.'

'Yes I do, I remember him from before the war,' says Mr Clagworth-Jones. 'Funny what you do remember. Not Munich, not the day the watermain burst, just an evening like this. We met on the corner out there and talked about how swallows gobble their prey in the air. Then the same happened to him. No reason at all.'

'Shall we all try a glass? We *do* have some for a wonder. He uses anything to hand,' she explains, 'to do his experiments in. Had I been houseproud, I would have been humbled.'

The first sip is wonderful. I thank her and say: 'It makes a nice change.' It's what my aunt – and mother come to that – say, an adult sort of thing quite seen through and yet brings a sort of security to say it. Why is Mr Clagworth-Jones always talking about my father? Norman lost his; mine being mislaid half the time is quite another thing from being extinguished in a Lancaster bomber.

'You kids no longer see,' he says, 'the old pop bottle stoppered by its own gas working against a glass marble. Work of genius, I used to think. Ideas come to you from the ether.'

'Is that where they come from?' asks Prunella. 'I've often wondered what to blame. When I was very small I did actually believe that children came from under gooseberry bushes. I used to look but never found one. But children are not the same as ideas.'

'Brainchildren is what people sometimes call ideas. What do you say, old son?'

'You have to have ideas for essays,' I say.

'"What I Did in the Holidays", I bet that's still one.'

'You can write about us,' says Prunella, ' and make us famous.'

'It's not yet real holidays. I just stay with my aunt from time to time when my parents go abroad.'

'Where are they now?'

'Norway or France I expect.'

Mr Clagworth-Jones has a sort of block of his pipe tobacco out on a bit of muslin cloth. He is slicing it carefully, all his size concentrated like the point of a heavy iron wedge. There is a silence around the task, around Prunella's beautiful, wistful, ageing face as I sit there holding my empty glass.

Then he says, 'I know who you are.' Then I wake. When will it stop?

New Titles from Flambard

PETER BENNET:	*All the Real*
ANDREA CAPES:	*Home Fires*
CYNTHIA FULLER:	*Moving Towards Light*
ANNA KAMIENSKA:	*Two Darknesses*
SHEONA LODGE:	*Swan Feather*
PETER MORTIMER:	*A Rainbow in its Throat*
CHRISTOPHER PILLING:	*Foreign Bodies*
PATRICIA POGSON:	*The Tides in the Basin*
MICHAEL STANDEN:	*Months and other stories*
MICHAEL STANDEN:	*Time's Fly-Past*
ALICIA STUBBERSFIELD:	*The Magician's Assistant*
FLAMBARD NEW POETS 1:	*Annie Foster, Fiona Hall, Caroline Smith*

Distributed by Password (Books) Ltd,
23 New Mount Street, Manchester M4 4DE.